THE MARZIPAN FRUIT BASKET

Copyright © 2017 Lucy E. M. Black

Except for the use of short passages for review purposes, no part of this book may be reproduced, in part or in whole, or transmitted in any form or by any means, electronically or mechanically, including photocopying, recording, or any information or storage retrieval system, without prior permission in writing from the publisher or a licence from the Canadian Copyright Collective Agency (Access Copyright).

 Canada Council for the Arts   Conseil des Arts du Canada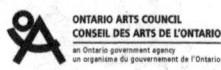

We gratefully acknowledge the support of the Canada Council for the Arts and the Ontario Arts Council for our publishing program. We also acknowledge the financial support of the Government of Canada through the Canada Book Fund.

Cover design: Val Fullard

The Marzipan Fruit Basket is a work of fiction. All the characters and situations portrayed in this book are fictitious and any resemblance to persons living or dead is purely coincidental.

Library and Archives Canada Cataloguing in Publication

Black, Lucy E. M., 1957-, author
    The marzipan fruit basket / short stories by Lucy E.M. Black.

(Inanna poetry & fiction series)
Issued in print and electronic formats.
ISBN 978-1-77133-377-1 (softcover). -- ISBN 978-1-77133-378-8 (epub).
-- ISBN 978-1-77133-379-5 (Kindle). -- ISBN 978-1-77133-380-1 (pdf)

    I. Title. II. Series: Inanna poetry and fiction series

PS8603.L2555M37 2017   C813'.6   C2017-900311-9
                                                                                       C2017-900312-7

Printed and bound in Canada

Inanna Publications and Education Inc.
210 Founders College, York University
4700 Keele Street, Toronto, Ontario M3J 1P3 Canada
Telephone: (416) 736-5356 Fax (416) 736-5765
Email: inanna.publications@inanna.ca Website: www.inanna.ca

THE MARZIPAN FRUIT BASKET

stories by
Lucy E. M. Black

inanna poetry & fiction series

INANNA PUBLICATIONS AND EDUCATION INC.
TORONTO, CANADA

For Michael and Andrew

Table of Contents

Silver
1

Local Woman Missing
6

South End
11

School Days
17

Maid of Honour
22

The Monkey House
27

The Wages of Sin
33

A Love Story
41

A Hawk in Winter
52

Oliver Hambley
58

Blue Eyes
68

The Yellow House
74

Blue Mountain
83

The Shoe Tree
86

The Whale Watcher
89

Gridlock
95

Roadside
98

Mrs. Harris
102

Romaine Hearts
106

The Canadian Shield
110

Creamers
116

Suzette's Garden
122

The Marzipan Fruit Basket
137

Garden Story
145

Acknowledgements
147

Silver

SILVER HAS A SWEET VOICE, delicate features, and dainty hands that sweep the air. Her dark hair is usually pulled up in a tight knot, and she walks upright with extended neck and carefully turned-out feet. Years of *pliés* and sweat at the *barre* have shaped her. She was named after the birch trees at the edge of the woods. People assumed that she was named Silver for her soft lyrical voice, but the name came before we heard the music in her.

On her fifth birthday, Gran bought her a ballet dress. It had several layers of tulle sewn onto a lycra body and a row of tiny sequins that ran along the shoulder straps and neckline. Mother helped her pull it on and adjusted the delicate fabric around her pudgy waist. "Now you must learn to tip toe," said Gran, "and when you can do that, I will pay for ballet lessons."

Father worked at the mine. He stayed with us for ten years before it shut down. I like to think that he wanted us to travel with him and to be a part of his new life, but I do not know if that is true. I remember him kneeling down and saying that he would always love us, and I remember the smell of his Old Spice. Mother did not come outside to see him leave. She cleaned the house when he was gone.

Silver is only sixteen and she is missing. When I look at her picture, I imagine that I still see the mark of her boyfriend's fingers. He is often rough with her. Once, when she was showering, I glimpsed shadowed bruises in green and yellow along the inside of her legs and was sickened by the sight of them. We warned her about Danny's temper, but she was in love. "It's only when he's depressed," she said, "when he feels that he's not getting anywhere."

We learned that Danny had quit Carleton's, where his job was to feed bark-covered logs through a ripsaw. He left town with his guitar and a knapsack the day before Silver disappeared. We were hopeful that she had gone after him. Danny O'Connell is in his twenties and works gigs at local bars crooning old Gordon Lightfoot songs. He can't hit the high notes, but it doesn't seem to matter much to the crowd. He looks great with dark shoulder-length hair, black jeans, a close-fitting shirt, and tight little ass. The audience always goes nuts, especially when they've had a few drinks. Their applause feeds his fantasies.

I waken from my sleep, damp and frightened. In my dream, the soft green calls me, and I begin, bare-footed, to step through a field. The clover resists the crushing feel of me, and I am sprung weightless above it, where I hover in the calm. The breezes gather to embrace me, and I am pushed forward gently, my arms stretched out to the dark sky. I am drawn to a thicket of bush where the shadows pull me further into the cool blackness. *I am coming for you*, I call. *I am waiting*, is carried back to me in the wind, and, in a rush of emotion, I start awake, filled with a heaviness that bears the loss and the grieving of her.

The police searched our homes and buildings. While they knocked on doors and poked through the secrets of our poverty, the men stalked the woods in organized sweeps. They said that the car would make locating her easy. She was last seen in a bar near the highway. It's a run-down shack that sells weed from the back door. I can't imagine why Silver would go there. The bartender said she came in with a townie and that they sat in the corner until three in the morning when he turned off the lights and left. He said Silver looked wasted and was slumped way down in the booth. He thought she would sleep it off and that he would find her there in the morning. It happens sometimes.

A few of the regulars said that the townie drove a tan pickup with a ram's head on the hood. They all said the truck looked pretty new and had a light bar on the roof and an old spotlight on the driver's side. The kind of stuff that assholes use to jack deer. He was in his thirties and slung his arm around Silver like they were an item. We asked the police to run license numbers for tan Dodge trucks, but they said there wasn't enough to go on.

A week after she went missing, the police found the car. It was burned out, but they could still read the VIN. It was off the highway on a stub road, about two hours from home. It was burned too badly for them to say if it had broken down or run out of gas. We waited for the rest. "Nobody inside," was what they said. "No signs of a body." My chest hurt from having held my breath.

After that I spoke to Gran. I told her about my dream and about floating through the woods until I heard Silver's voice. She said it must be a sign and that our connection was so strong that Silver was summoning me. I borrowed some cash and a van and drove to the city.

I camped in the first hotel room for three days. Each morning I rose, showered in the rust-stained cubicle, and drank bad coffee made with hot tap water and a jar of instant. In the evenings, I walked the entertainment strip hoping for a glimpse of her. I went to the ballet studio and talked with her teachers and other dancers. Everyone said she would be found if she wanted to be found. Runaways are common.

I had the dream again last night but did not hear my sister's voice. When I phoned home, my mother cried. She is afraid that we will both become lost. She told me that she heard an owl hooting in the night, a sign of death. I promised to find

Silver, and I promised to return with her soon. When I hung up the phone, I was filled with shame because I felt inadequate for the task.

I didn't have a plan, only a strong sense that I must move quickly to find her. I drove west, stopping only to use the rest stations briefly and to sleep in the van. Early this morning, I arrived in Kitwanga and pulled over to look at the mountain peaks. The season is changing. The greens have dulled since I left home and taken on a tired brown. The morning air was cold, and I had to turn on the window defroster. A pair of osprey circled overhead, and I squinted to look at them. Another warning sign. Instinctively, I locked the doors, breathing quickly, my stomach heaving, and started to drive again, far too fast at first, fishtailing away from the gravel shoulder.

I have tried hard to find Danny. First, I believed that he was still on the road, chasing his dreams, and then that he had found work in another saw mill. I imagined him bending over a log somewhere, with gloved hands, whistling to himself while the blade spins hungrily, spewing chewed bits of wood into the air. He is coated in a dusting of wet wood, with the cavities in his nostrils lightly powdered. His eyelashes blink repeatedly to remove fine residue. There is a streak of sweat down his back, building a light orange strip of damp sawdust. His jagged fingernails are blackened from the sharp edges of bark ripping at them through his sodden gloves. But then I imagine him greased and oiled for a show somewhere, his hair tied back in a sleek ponytail, his jeans pressed and waiting for him to struggle into.

It is Silver that I can't see. Is she in a hotel room somewhere waiting for him to return, or is she curled in a small ball sleeping securely, her tummy pumping air in a child-like rhythm? Are they together, or is someone else keeping her from us? These thoughts come to me and I am filled with panic. I stop driving and get out and kneel at the side of the road. I gather a handful of earth and inhale its fragrance. It is dry like the season.

There is no promise of life in this soil, just the whiff of decay. I remain kneeling until a large truck passes. Embarrassed, I stand up quickly, brushing the dust from my knees.

Local Woman Missing

THE HEADLINE IN THE LOCAL PAPER caught my attention. *Local Woman Missing. Annie Prosser, thirty-eight, was last seen Friday night on Regional Road 59. Prosser is described as 5'8" with shoulder-length brown hair, wearing a purple jacket.* I often noticed her striding out of the village early in the morning with a brown vinyl purse swinging by her side. I put down the newspaper and looked out my kitchen window. Miles of rich, rolling farmland spread in every direction. I am safe here in the openness and light.

Ladybug! Ladybug! Fly away home. We recited this as children when we saw a ladybug, and then we'd puff air on it to help with its flight. There were little ladybugs stitched inside the label of my underwear as a child. "Show me the ladybug," he'd say, pulling me close. "I want to see the ladybugs."

Ashdon has been my home for six years. We moved from the city. My husband's job in international finance allowed him to work largely from home. The house was a ruin, far worse than we had been led to believe by either the agent or the home inspector. The mice, chipmunks, raccoons, and bats were unhappy with our arrival, and we spent several months establishing ourselves as the dominant species. All of the money we had set aside for special projects was quickly absorbed by the structural work. Groups of contractors moved in when we did. Buckets of tools and stacks of materials were deposited in all of the rooms that I had tidied, in what turned out to be a futile attempt to carve out a small, calm, living space.

And then, unexpectedly, my husband announced that he found himself, "out of love" with me. He blurted this out at breakfast. While he finished eating, I went to our newly painted bedroom and packed him a suitcase. I wasn't angry, particularly. I was mostly full of wondering. And so he left, and I, having seen the house at its most vulnerable, felt obliged to stay and finish alone what we had started together.

My father's voice: you are so stupid and so ugly, it's no wonder he left you.

I was in our village gas station/post-office/convenience store last week when I saw that someone had tacked up a picture of Annie. "She was young then," said Millie, "married with a real nice little boy. They had a house in Ramsey. He must be seventeen by now. The boy. You have no idea'r," continued Millie, "how her mother suffered. The woman ought to be given a medal. I couldn't do it," she declared. She nodded at me for emphasis, her chin tilting up and down, like a small glass woodpecker I once had that bobbed to drink from the edge of a cup. I stood there and waited, knowing that if I were patient she would fill the space between us with story. Millie leaned across the counter and began.

"Lydia Prosser was teachering in the city. Taught in one of them schools with foreigners and the like. She got herself mixed up with a fella' who come from family with coin and they didn't hold no truck with her. And so Lydia and him came here and didn't he just up and die before the baby was born. Well then, his family won't have no never-mind with the girl and she's all by herself, and the proud thing just about froze herself to death the first winter. That's how come it be that her daughter, Annie, came out as strange as ever. Always running after a puff of cloud or a bit of wind, and the fellas hangin' around her like moths to a flame, and Lydia not knowing how to keep her safe. Finally, one day, Doc Webb says as he's heard that there's a place in the city that can help with such a child, and so Lydia takes her there and then they puts electricity to her head. She comes home a few months later, calm as a dove but with no more sparkle, and she marries a Culham, has a boy, and then goes all strange again." Millie pulled away from me to eye the effect.

"Yes," I said, "it's very sad."

"Men have urges," my mother had once said by way of explanation. "They can't help themselves. You must learn not to provoke him." But I would not learn. I fought every touch. I hid from him when he called, and I cursed him when he began to scratch his calloused fingers along my bare arms and legs.

I was in the front garden one afternoon when Earl drove by in his pick-up and waved at me. Earl had been kind, doing all sorts of useful repairs when things broke or simply stopped working. All he would ever take for his trouble was a cup of coffee and a piece of pie. Even when I said there was no rush, and that I didn't want to take him out of his way, he'd trundle over after milking "the girls." Hands in his overall pockets, he'd nod at me and say, "Thought I'd see what was what." When he was done his small chore, he would say, "Well, that's all right for now then," and stand there awkwardly, waiting for me to offer the exchange.

Alone, in the quiet, I can sometimes feel myself cringing with the recollection of his voice and the violence of his hands.

Days later, I saw a small dark object ahead of me in the gloaming. Perhaps an animal or a piece of debris. I slowed the Audi, braking tentatively. As I drew near, I saw that it was a small huddled figure. I stopped my car and put on the hazards. She turned to look at me when I opened my door.

"My bag is empty," she said. "They told me to wait for more."

Don't wait. Hide. Disappear. For God's sake, don't draw attention to yourself.

"Who told you that, Annie?" I asked. Speaking quietly,

standing far away so as not to frighten her. "Who told you?"

"Fuck you, you cock-sucking whore, you son-of-a-bitch fuck-headed old bag."

I moved further back and waited.

"You have no appointment," Annie continued, "and therefore the judge requires you in accordance with a marriage from which point it might be possible."

"I can take you home now," I offered, "to your mother."

"I'm marled," she responded, "and the sky is turning again."

"Please come," I encouraged, "I'll get you a nice cup of tea."

"I only take raisins, you see. They told me that," she answered.

She was jittery in the car, fidgeting with the window controls and pulling at the seatbelt. It was a short drive to the Prosser house. I turned into the lane, and Annie jumped out, leaving the door ajar. I put the car in park and got out to shut her door. By the time I had done so, she had run off, disappearing behind one of the outbuildings.

I drove to the cemetery months after my father's death and touched the letters of our shared name on the cold stone. Then I cried. But it was with sheer relief.

I walked to the side door and knocked loudly. Old farm equipment was discarded in the yard, and the remnants of a rusted stove and ringer washing machine were nearby. Mrs. Prosser came to the door wearing a thin cotton housedress and a flowered apron. Her grey hair was loose around her face and shoulders. Most of the local matrons wore their hair cut short, barbered and permed, or pulled tightly into unforgiving little buns. "Yes'm," she said by way of greeting.

"Mrs. Prosser," I began, "I picked up Annie. She ran over there." I pointed between the large banked barn and the drive shed.

"Thankee, then," she replied, "I best be after her."

I stepped back from the door, expecting her to come outside and to join me, but she stepped backwards instead. Into the darkness. I stood there stupidly for a moment before leaving.

My father shadows me. Taunting and criticizing. When my husband left, and when the contractors finished, I was alone in a big, empty house. And his voice found me there. Whispering behind the walls.

South End

"FUCK YOU, YOU FUCKIN' CRUSTY FUCKER." An eloquence of fucks. Adjective. Verb. Noun. There was an English lesson in there somewhere. She was fifteen and suspended from school. Irony.

Her teacher was, according to Summer, "a fuckin' perv," but the real reason for skipping was a shift change. At three o'clock, the lines formed at the east gate, past the wooden security shack and the twelve-foot-high fencing with barbed wire. The line snaked back, curled around the plant, engines running, while the short-of-breath security guard, in a grey Stainmaster shirt and pants, checked the truck beds and trunks, searching for stolen bumpers and hand tools. The line could take forty-five minutes to clear. "They're all fuck'in pervs. They like it when I jump in and show them my tits. For a twenty, I go down on them, and they don't lose their place. I pull my hair back. They like that. Short skirts and T-shirts with no bra. Makes 'em hard. I can do five in a row easy. Then I puke it up. Bet you can't make no fuckin' hunered bucks in half'en hour."

She was in Grade Nine.

I was shocked to discover that thirty minutes from my safe, middle-class life, people lived in such circumstances. No hydro. No water. Whole families squatting in abandoned buildings. Street kids sleeping in wrecked cars. Kids coming to school in deep winter without coats or boots, sitting at their desks with bleeding gums and teeth loose from scurvy.

Summer was a survivor. She had already found a way to look after herself. The monthly cheque her mother received paid the rent and a few bills. There was never enough left for a full month of food. It was her mother who had sent Summer to "work." Told her where to find the men and what to say to them. How to swallow.

Summer and I had one standoff. I had attempted to chastise her for not making school a priority. "Fuck you, bitch," she snapped. Her blue eyes focused on me intently. She moved her tiny child-like body right up to me, the smell of her strong and feral, placing her feet apart in a firm stance. She clenched her small fists and spat at me, "You just don't fuckin' get it!" We would have looked ridiculous to a passer-by. Me, the authority, dressed in a flowered summer dress, stepping backwards from the girl, who was all of ninety pounds, menacing and ready to pounce.

She left school in early October. I was patrolling the smoking area at lunch when a battered black limousine pulled up; they were recruiting workers to harvest weed up north. She seemed to be expecting the summons and jumped in without hesitation. She yelled to a couple of others and they climbed in as well. "See you in two weeks," one of them cheerfully called out while pulling the door shut. I tried to get the license plate number, but there didn't seem to be one.

We attempted to phone their homes but the phone numbers were out of service and the addresses bogus. It was not uncommon to discover that many of our students listed the local convenience store as their mailing address. We notified the police department, but, in truth, no crime had yet been committed. They were not missing. They were "employed." This was not, I was told, an atypical disappearance.

There was a biker clubhouse to the east of us, and, when they were having a membership meeting, they would swing by the school and collect a dozen girls, offering them free modelling lessons. Drugged and costumed, the girls would be used as dancers and live entertainment. The lucky ones might make it back a week later. Others, more susceptible to the crack-laced pot, would develop an affinity for the drug that would keep them captive.

Some of the girls told Jade this when they returned and she, in turn, told me. "The guys in the black limo, miss, are messed. They're all fuckin' whacked. They don't give two shits about nobody. They all got fuckin' tats from prison. Tears for every sonofabitch they killed. Two or three each. And tattooed shit crawling up their necks. They're fuckin' psycho. There are girls locked in rooms in the basement. You gotta' tell people to stay away from that limo."

Jade was my source. If something was about to go down anywhere in the school, she would give me a heads-up. It wasn't that she expected me to do anything about it; she just wanted me to know that she was connected. I respected this.

Jade aspired to dance at the Dynasty, a local hang-out for guys on the line, where sixteen-year-old girls could jump on a table and earn whatever money was shoved into their costumes. The costumes themselves didn't have to be fancy—laced leather skirts, bikini tops, and strappy heels would do. Sometimes the girls wore their outfits to school and were indignant when I made them cover up with a T-shirt.

I tried to tell Jade that there was more to life. That she could go to college and work anywhere she wanted. She scoffed. College was not part of her world. She was vociferous in her contempt for my prim sanctimony. She showed me her tracks and the tiny puncture marks between her toes. I learned to abbreviate my lectures, curtail my judgment, and to laugh a little.

"K, miss, like what the fuck do I need to know that shit for? Ya' think some Joe's gonna come up to me and say, "Yo, Jade, like can you show me how to fuckin' calculate the circumference of a cylinder. No way, Miss. It's just a bunch of fuckin' useless bullshit."

Although she was only fifteen, she had things to do, places to go, money to earn. If she dropped by the school three or four times a week, attending two or three classes a day, that was a concession. A good-faith demonstration that conceded a willingness to credit that *maybe* there was something to learn. As long as we didn't, "just fuckin' waste her time."

One afternoon, as the bell rang, our doors were pushed open and streams of teenagers escaped from the building, running purposefully to the front field. A car pulled up, and a young man I did not know jumped out with a length of pipe in one hand and a knife in the other. I ran toward the crowd that was quickly forming. They broke apart respectfully when I reached them, and I stepped forward into the ring. One of our students, a tough grade-ten boy, lay in the grass curled into a foetal position, his arm slashed and his face and head badly beaten. The attacker escaped in the waiting car. The boy was in shock. I radioed the office for an ambulance. The onlookers stood back, watching me.

"What happened?" I screamed at them. "Who did this? Tell me what just happened here!" But they were all quiet and avoided eye contact with me. The victim couldn't or wouldn't speak either. "Is this what you want?" I yelled. "Do you want this violence at school? Tell me what happened!" They stepped backwards, away from my anger, and the crowd thinned quickly, leaving me alone in the centre of the field with the wounded boy.

A couple of days later, Jade dropped by my office. "It was a set-up, Miss. A beating-in. He had to prove himself."

I was incredulous. "You mean he *knew* the attackers? He could have been killed."

"Yeah, sure. But now he's safe. He belongs. He made it to the first level. He's protected now."

"What do you mean, the first level? What gang is this?"

"I'm not sayin'. Miss, there's some shit you shouldn't know."

"Why not?"

"'Cause they're fuckin' all over, that's why. And they'd mess me up if they thought I was talkin' smack about them."

"What's the first level? What does that mean?"

"It's like beginner. To work your way up, you gotta do shit. Bad shit. And then you move up."

"What kind of bad shit, Jade?"

"You know, small stuff. Rob a store. Steal a car."

"And then what happens?"

"Then, you become trusted. More powerful. Then you have to gang-bang a chick. And the last thing is you whack someone. That's all I know."

I was silent. And she was scared. Just telling me these things had subdued her.

"Ya' gotta be careful, Miss. There's a lot you don't know. You can't mess with this shit."

I could not help but wonder what Jade would be like if she attended another school, lived in another community. At fifteen, she was dressed like the tough, south-end chick she was. Her hair was shoulder-length and carefully curled into soft, big waves. She wore thick foundation with elaborate eye makeup, intense red lip gloss, and glitter on her cheekbones. Tight jeans and a deeply unbuttoned, sheer black blouse made up her look. It suited her. But sometimes, I just wanted to scrub her face and see what would happen. I wondered what it would take to get her to college. "You can be so much more than this," I had repeatedly told all of them. "You can be anything you want to be."

"Hey Miss," Jade beckoned to me one day in the hallway, "I met this really cool guy, he's going to look after me."

I don't remember my exact response, but it was likely something prim and unenthusiastic, "Well I hope he wants you to graduate."

"This is it!" she announced about a month later. She had dropped into my office, and was perched on the edge of my desk. "You'll be glad to know, I'm fuckin' done. Checkin' out.

Gonna have a kid. You're not goin' to have to mess with me no more."

"A baby?" I repeated stupidly. "Are you getting married, Jade?"

"Fuck, no!" she said, "I'm gonna be a baby momma. He don't gotta marry me for that."

"But Jade," I protested, "you're so smart. You could do so much with your life."

"An' I'm *doin'* it, bitch. Don't you see? It's workin' out. I'm gonna have my own kid. I get paid to have kids. Lots of *beootiffal* babies."

My protests and sadness were left unspoken. Instead I looked at her. She was smiling at me, looking happy and confident. This was something she could do. It was something that made sense to her.

School Days

WHEN CARLA WALKS through the classroom door, I welcome her and pass her the handouts she needs. Her arms are scarred by the cuts she herself has made. The other students sense her distrust. I become entirely aware of her, softening my speech and establishing a quieted tone. Despite my best efforts, she bolts from the room long before the bell rings. I relax to see her leave, but then am engulfed with a sense of shame, and run after her to the nearby washroom. She cowers in the corner, hands over her face, trembling like a wild creature caught.

I look in the mirror and I see my sister's face. She was lovely: exotic with long lashes and a sensual energy that earned her *a reputation*. She was suspended from school repeatedly. "Willful." "Disrespectful." "Lazy." "Careless." "Rude." These words formed her legacy. I was looked at disapprovingly by the teachers when I first began Junior High. I was *the younger one*. They waited for me to demonstrate my familial failings, my bad blood.

I needed to be silent and unnoticed. To slouch in my seat and be passed over, to shelter in the library or an empty hallway at lunch.

On the first day of class, Mr. Hawkins took attendance and moved me from an unobtrusive spot at the back to front-row centre. "I knew your sister," he intoned, "and I'll have none of that again." I shuffled forward while my classmates peered with interest. The hallways echoed with his unkind words for weeks afterwards, as the boys parroted him. I took refuge in the stairwell until I calculated that they had grown bored and moved away.

We began the second day of class with an introduction to Shakespeare. My classmates struggled to stay awake. I was rapt. Leaning forward, I took down in tiny script everything that Hawkins said. The poetry and the structure of the play were breathtaking. Too quickly, the class was over and we were dismissed for lunch. I was in a daze. I had never encountered anything like it. It was masterful. And this hateful man had opened a world to me without acknowledging any sense of awe.

I was called upon to read a long soliloquy by Cassius. I read well. I did not stop at the end of my page but continued through until the end of the speech. Then I sat down. Triumphant. "Pride, Miss Maccarone, goeth before a fall," Mr. Hawkins pronounced.

Our first book report was due by the end of the month. The other girls in the class handed in their reports with wool bows tied through the holes of the three-ring paper, and little daisy chains decorating their title pages. Mine was neatly typed and stapled together in the top left-hand corner. The following Monday we received our papers back. Mine had a large "D-" written in red pencil. There was no explanation. No commentary. My face burned. I waited until the class was dismissed and I stood facing him. My knees were knocking. "Why?" I simply asked him, holding out my paper.

"You could *not possibly* have read that book," he sneered. "You obviously plagiarized the report from the book cover or from someone else. I don't like cheaters." He gathered his notes, slid them into a leather valise, and walked out of the classroom. I was too ashamed to tell anyone.

I wondered what my sister had done to incur such hatred.

He exacted upon me every cutting thing within his power. He allowed the boys to heckle and make jokes in class about *Wops*.

He himself made disparaging remarks about immigrants and their inability to appreciate good literature. "Literature" was pronounced "Lit-ra-chure." He signalled, in this way, permission for further ridicule, and the boys responded by calling out "brown-noser" when I raised my hand. He barked my name only when I had chosen not to participate. I would jump to my feet, responding smartly when prompted. It incensed him and I could see his neck go blotchy with rage. He diminished my answers with vague comments like, "yes, *you would* think that," which produced nervous giggles from the rest of the room. Similarly, my marked tests and essays were savaged. Half marks taken off everywhere for undefined "errors."

I imagined my sister in Grade Seven or Eight, before she was removed from school. Leaning across his desk seductively. Brushing up against him. Arousing him. And then calling him a *freak* with disdain. She *must* have done something like that.

In Grade Ten, I started high school. English was held in a large classroom in the academic wing. Perched on a stool under a spotlight, the room in shadows, was Mr. Amos. We filed in self-consciously and slid into seats. He waited until we were settled and then opened a book and began to read to us. Poetry. *Ode on a Grecian Urn*. His voice resonating beautifully. His tone rich. His pacing impeccable.

He saw at once that I was entranced. He passed me *Heart of Darkness* to read while the rest of the class plodded through *Jonathan Livingston Seagull*. He took me aside and encouraged me to think about Conrad's journey, his exploration of human nature. He pushed me to think. My friends teased me. They misunderstood entirely.

My father gave me a gold cross and chain on my sixteenth birthday. He said that girls didn't need an education; it was time to get a job. I bowed my head and did not look at him. "Yes, Papa."

I walked to the school office to tell them I was withdrawing. They called Mr. Amos. He told me that I was a gifted student.

I should go to university, he said. There were scholarships available. I could spend four years working on an English degree—reading books. The guidance counsellor offered to call my parents. I stayed at school for the remainder of the day.

My parents were waiting for me in the dining room when I got home. I summoned courage and went to them. My father was angry. "'Dey called fum 'de school," he began, "an' 'den dey tol' me, I haf no right. I haf a right!" he bellowed.

"I'm sorry, Papa," I interjected, "I didn't mean for them to call." I was shaking. Afraid of what might come next.

"You stay 'der," he yelled, "'til June. But no calls to my work. Unerstan'?" He took his arm and swept the tablecloth and dinner plates off the table. Everything crashed to the floor. "Clean 'dis shit!" he roared.

My mother helped me. I slunk down the hall and went to bed without dinner. I avoided him for days. I kept my head down at mealtime. My sister was delighted. For once she was not the centre of the storm. I saw her embracing him while he watched the evening news. She stood behind his chair and slid her arms around this neck, bending herself forward to put her cheek next to his.

I discovered the New Canadian Library series. Margaret Laurence. Morley Callaghan. Hugh MacLennan. Gabrielle Roy. Stephen Leacock. I read all of them. After work one night, I took two buses to the university and picked up an admissions package. I applied as a mature student. Without a grade thirteen diploma, it was my only option.

And then came the horrible part. I approached my parents one night when my sister was at a party. Boldly. I entered the living room with my acceptance letter and handed it to him. "I'm going to university," I said. "They have accepted me."

My father was stunned. Choked silent while he absorbed and processed the information. He stood up and came towards me. "You can no do it!" he erupted. "Girls don' go." But I was resolved. He was violent. Smashing things. Threatening.

"I dare you," I said, "go ahead. Hit me. You don't own me!"

He towered over me, the veins raised on his temples, his fists clenched. I waited for the blow, but it did not happen. I opened my eyes. He spit in my face and cursed me. He pushed me hard against the wall so that I smashed my head and saw swirls of black and gold. My vision blurred. He left the house.

"What have you done?" my mother cried. "Oh, what have you done?"

I walk to Carla quietly and put my arms around her, pulling her gently into the safety of my embrace. I hold her and do not speak. I cannot protect her for long.

Maid of Honour

MY DAUGHTER WANTS TO LOOK at my wedding pictures, but I prefer to keep the album safely tucked away. Mixed memories are hard to explain, especially when she turns the plastic pages to the wedding party, posed self-consciously on a staircase in an old, grand house rented for the occasion and, particularly, when she asks me about my maid of honour.

I met my maid of honour, Maria, in university. She wore glossy lipstick, tight jeans, and a deeply cut top, all of which contrasted sharply with the casual athletic clothing worn by everyone else. I noticed her mannerisms first: fingers splayed and hands held away from her body in gestures of helplessness. She seemed entirely out of sync with the burgeoning feminism around us. I wondered if she was a graduate student plant, one of the unending experiments taking place all over campus to monitor social behaviour. (One afternoon while crossing a courtyard, I observed a large crowd watching a young man have an epileptic seizure. "Don't call 911," someone shouted authoritatively. "It's just another Zimbardo stunt.") But, over lattes, sipped standing up against a grimy counter, I was disarmed by her and began to believe that she was consciously trying to find herself.

My other friends didn't like her. They left the pub when I walked in with her, always claiming that they were just on their way somewhere else. As far as I could tell, their dislike wasn't grounded in any particular offence, only a general unease. Maria, however, was a really good listener who also asked penetrating questions. Although she rarely divulged anything about herself, she was extremely interested in every aspect of my life—and the lives of my friends.

I pushed her once to tell me something about her own past. Very reluctantly, she began to talk, her face flushed and her eyes hard. She only gave me fragments. She told me that her second cousin had always been a good friend. While together at a wedding, he drank too much and forced himself on her. Afterwards he threw up and drove her home. The next day he sent flowers. A couple of days later he came to the house with an engagement ring. She found out from her younger sister that he was telling people that he was "obligated" to marry Maria. In a fury, she broke off the engagement.

I sometimes found her behaviour unnerving. While walking, for instance, we'd pass someone and she'd say, "Don't turn around, he's following us." And then she'd lead us on a bizarre route to our destination, all the while describing the ways in which he had either "creeped her out" or "undressed her with his eyes."

When we graduated, Maria went on to do an MBA, and I took a marketing job. We lived in different parts of the city, but stayed in touch. She called me three or four times a week and grilled me about the minutiae of my life. Where did I have lunch? Who did I eat it with? What was I wearing? What was new at work? She seemed intent on maintaining our connection. In turn, she told me about the men she was seeing—including her sexual exploits—although all of the relationships seemed to be short-lived.

I had been dating a journalist. Maria hated him and continued to enumerate all of his shortcomings: "He's too old. He's boring. He's overweight. You can do better." After a short conversation on the phone with her, I'd sometimes allow myself to be drawn in. Afterwards, I would find myself fighting with him. "You don't appreciate me. You take me for granted. You don't respect me." Groundless stuff that came out in her voice and totally bewildered him.

Maria lived in a small bachelor loft, an almost entirely empty, white box. A desk and a bed and a pile of business texts comprised the extent of her décor. She was uninterested in making it comfortable, preferring to spend all of her money on clothes. One night while visiting, Maria left off criticizing my boyfriend and surprised me with a question: "Do you ever masturbate? Like really get into it?"

"Why?"

"I'm really good at it," she responded. "I can make myself come in two minutes. I know just where to touch."

There were always questions for me. Where did I shop for antiques? She had a friend who wanted to know. What was the name of my favourite perfume? She wanted to buy it for her sister. What was that store I liked for funky jewellery? She wanted to get something as a gift for a friend. Where was my favourite restaurant? She needed to take someone out for lunch. The lists of questions lasted for weeks.

In the meantime, after a year of dating, Scott proposed. We kept it low-key until after we had gone to Pittsburgh to visit his family. I put off telling Maria, afraid of her reaction. Finally, when I did tell her, she didn't seem all that surprised. "I'm going to be the maid of honour," she announced. "I've never been one before."

The necessity of sharing wedding plans with Maria gave us a renewed sense of intimacy, and I found myself slipping into old routines. I told her things that, later, I wished that I had not. And she, in turn, continued to obsess about the tiniest details of my life. What store did we order the couch from? What was the name of the colour we were painting the dining room? Where did we buy our rug?

Looking back now, I see that another stage had begun. Mostly, our wedding day was a happy blur. But Maria arrived wearing flashy gold silk and looking like she had been out all night. Her hair was wild, and the dress was stained and wrinkled. She told me that she'd been to another wedding the night before and had worn the dress to "break it in." She hadn't been home to shower or freshen up. I was upset, but was told to "get over myself." Later, when everyone was kissing us goodbye, she went up to Scott and kissed him full on the lips, clinging to him for just a little too long. It shocked us.

After the wedding, I was deliberately cool with her. I abbreviated my telephone conversations and claimed to be busy when I was not. Later, I felt sorry that I had not been more sympathetic. After work one night, I picked up some take-out and drove to her place for a surprise visit. She could not have been more unexcited to see me. When she finally let me in, I was astonished to notice that she had completely redecorated. Everything looked like ours—the same colours, the same couch, the same rug, the same china, the same shower curtain. Everything had been duplicated. I tried not to stare. In an effort to compose myself, I entered the bathroom. On a hunch, I opened the medicine cabinet. Inside was my perfume, my hair-blower, and my brand of make-up. Every detail duplicated.

When I rejoined her, I said, "You've done a lot since I was last here. Everything looks brand new."

"Yes," she replied, avoiding eye contact. "I decided that if I was going to bring men home, it should look like someone really lived here. I loved your couch so much that I ordered the same one. I hope you don't mind."

"No, of course not. Imitation is the highest form of flattery."

"I guess so. Let's go out for drinks."

We walked to a nearby café. Maria told me about a prof at grad school and the hot sex they were having in his office, late at night. I was glad when she excused herself to go to the ladies room. Alone at the table, I noticed that her over-sized bag held a number of journals I assumed contained study notes for her exams. I selected one. The first page was titled "Music," and listed my favourite artists and performers. Page two was titled "Books," and listed my favourite books. Page three, "Art." Page four, "Food." On it went. I slipped the book back into her bag, my hands trembling. I had been catalogued.

When I told Scott what I had seen, his reaction was instantaneous. "She's completely fucked up. She's your friend and I won't tell you what to do, but keep her away from me. I don't trust her."

She continued to call and to ask me personal questions. Although I was unwilling to see her, I did answer her questions. I was afraid to confront her. Eventually, my other friends convinced me to change my cell number. She called me at work. It was an angry screaming attack that accused me of betraying and abandoning her. She continued to call. Pleading sometimes. Profanity and threats at other times. She would show me what a bastard Scott was. How he'd turned me against her. How he'd come on to her at a party. She could have him if she wanted.

In desperation, I counter-attacked. I told her that she was sick and needed help. I said that she needed to find her own life and that she *had* to leave me alone. I threatened to call the police if she continued to harass me. She shrieked into the phone, a loud high-pitched animal scream. Silently, I hung up.

Over the years, I threw out all of the photographs of us together except for the ones at my wedding when she was my maid of honour. Sometimes, I worry that she is still, from a distance, monitoring my life.

The Monkey House

SHE WAS SUPPOSED TO HOLD MY HAND, Mother said. As soon as we went inside, she let go. I stood still. I was a scaredy-cat. She said so. She went over to the first of the cells. I took a few small steps forward, but the screaming stopped me. And the smell. It was a bad smell. I didn't know what to do. I couldn't run back outside because they would all laugh at me. And I couldn't stay there. It was a bad place.

My sister was pounding the window with the palm of her hand and yelling. The monkeys screamed back at her. She laughed at them. There were three of them. Two on a tree branch stuck in the concrete and another one by a small puddle of water on the floor. They were all staring at her. She was wearing red cotton shorts and a blouse with little red apples printed on it. Maybe they wanted to eat the apples, I thought. Do monkeys eat apples? Would they break the glass and grab her? I looked at my shorts. They were green. My blouse had green and yellow stripes on it. I was safe. They wouldn't eat stripes. I took another step.

My sister began to jump up and down. She waved her arms and screamed. I looked at the monkeys. They were mad at her. She moved to the next room. The walls were painted yellow, and there were trees painted in green and brown on the back wall. Ropes hung from the ceiling. The monkeys were swinging on the ropes. My sister walked past them.

I looked carefully before moving forward. The cement floor

was slippery. I was cold and needed to go to the bathroom.

She stopped at the next one. It had the scary baboons. They were scratching. My sister leaned over and put her bottom against the glass. She scratched under her arms and in her hair. She wiggled her bum at them. She laughed at them and called out. Wiggling and scratching. They watched her and screamed. They got mad too. They ran at her and threw themselves on the glass; they bounced back on the floor and did it again. She kept wiggling and scratching. They screamed and screamed at her. The noise was echoing and the other monkeys were screaming too. It was really loud.

She didn't even wait for me before leaving. I took a few more steps and hurried past the baboons. There was a black chimp on his own in the next little room. It was painted blue and had white clouds painted along the top. There was a car tire and a piece of dirty material on the floor. My sister made a face and stuck her lips and chin out. The chimp watched her and then pulled the material over his face. She pulled her blouse out of her shorts and pulled it up over her face. Her boobies showed. I looked around to make sure no one else was there to see. We were alone.

"You better stop," I said. "Mom will be mad."

"Aww, baby going to tattle-tale?"

"I am not a baby!"

She turned around and looked at me. She still had her blouse pulled up to her chin and her boobies were still showing. She lifted her top up and down at me. "Don't!" I said.

She laughed at me. "Scaredy-cat, scaredy-cat!" she sneered. I was really sad now. And I had to go to the bathroom badly. There were still more rooms to pass before reaching the exit.

"Hurry up," I said. "I have to go number one."

"Baby going to wet her pants cause she's a scaredy-cat."

"I am not!"

I tried to move closer to her but she stepped backwards, away from me.

She told my mother that we had to leave because I had to go to the bathroom. She held my hand tightly and walked me to the washrooms. They smelled too. My mother was happy with her for taking care of me.

On the way out, she pushed me up close to the snake aquarium. A brown boa constrictor was looped around a branch, sleeping. She said she'd feed me to the snake if I tattled, and that he'd wrap himself around my neck and squeeze so hard he'd crush me to death and swallow me in one bite.

She told me other things too. That if I was bad, spiders would crawl into my hair when I was sleeping and make a nest and burrow down to my brain and their babies would crawl out of my ears. Outside, she told me that the squirrels had rabies. And that she knew how to make them bite me. And that I would foam at the mouth and go crazy and they'd have to shoot me to death.

I didn't tell on her. I didn't tell when she jumped on top of me and tried to smother me with a pillow. I didn't tell when she walked me to Sunday school and left me there alone and went to Dairy Queen. And I didn't tell when she climbed out of our bedroom window and went to the Red Barn for a hamburger at night-time when we were supposed to be asleep.

And one day, when she and her friend, Rodney, climbed on our garage roof and pelted people with plums from our tree, and my mother asked me if I knew anything about it, I said that Rodney did it, and he got in trouble but she didn't. But that didn't make her glad. She still called me a rat.

I was always a baby or a rat or a scaredy-cat.

She was beautiful. People always said how pretty she was. And daring. She was the only one I knew who was brave enough to do the stuff she did. Her friends dared her to do stuff and she did it. She stole lipstick from the store once. She said bad words. She was rude. She wouldn't help do the dishes. She left the backyard even when she was grounded. She spit.

She dropped out of school at sixteen and worked at part-time jobs in hairdressing salons and convenience stores. None of those jobs ever lasted beyond one pay cheque. As soon as she got paid, she did something and got fired. And then she spent all of her money on makeup and nail polish. And when she ran out of money, she looked for another job. My parents stopped giving her allowance. But that didn't matter. I saw her once, sneaking money out of my mother's handbag.

As quickly as she was able to secure jobs and make new friends, she also shrugged them off. I watched in admiration as she navigated her teen years, collecting and rejecting boyfriends, in turn. She enumerated their attributes for me while she readied herself for a date. One was a good dancer, another made her laugh, there was one with a good job, someone with a nice car, a good kisser, a smart dresser. These were the features she held in high regard.

She married at eighteen. He was an okay kisser, with a good job, and a nice car. A winning combination. She wore a pink wool suit and pointy silver shoes, and her hair was teased and sprayed into a mound of soft curls. They married at City Hall and drove to Niagara Falls for their honeymoon. The marriage was short-lived. She was home within the year and started dating again. When I asked her why, she told me that her ex-husband had eczema and she couldn't stand the dry skin that flaked off all over her.

Her thirst for all things new seemed insatiable. Her short time as a wife had not domesticated her, and she reverted to doing her own thing while our mother did her laundry and made her bed. Her ex-husband provided spending money, so she did not feel the need to find a job. Instead, she partied, slept in late, and continued to focus on her appearance, her wardrobe, and her beauty regimes. And the rest of us were complicit. Dazzled by her.

One day, before my mother even had a chance to wear it herself, she took my mother's new winter coat. Cherry red wool with a grey lamb's wool collar. She didn't ask. Just put it on and went out. My mother said nothing to her. When the door shut, I looked at my mother and asked if she minded.

"Of course not," she said, "it looks good on her. Too fancy for me anyway. She can keep it now." And my mother continued to wear her shabby brown coat instead.

I believed in magic and fairies and wishes long past the time when such things were encouraged. Unlike the others, she did not actively scorn my make-belief.

"Imagine," I once pondered, "if the fairies came into my room when I was sleeping and tidied up all of my Barbies for me."

"You should try it, and see," she suggested.

And so that night, instead of tidying my dolls and their extensive wardrobe and furniture as I had been instructed by my mother, I went to bed with all of the my play still strewn around the room in a whirlwind of mess. When I awoke the next morning, everything had been tidily packed away and my room was in pristine condition. In the centre of my desk was a piece of paper with the tiniest of printing on it. It was a note from the Blue Fairy who had visited my room and tidied it. I was ecstatic and showed everyone my letter from Fairyland. No one else in the house shared in my excitement. My father suggested that the note looked suspicious and had perhaps been forged. I was devastated by his disbelief.

That night, I once again crept into bed leaving my books and toys in disarray. I pulled the covers over my head and peeked out into the room, determined to stay awake for my fairy visitor. The need for sleep overcame my desire to remain awake, and I drifted off. For a second time when I awoke, my room had been magically restored. This time, however, there was no note. Ebullient, I skipped through the house proclaiming my good news. The Blue Fairy had once again visited.

As bedtime beckoned, I became reckless with my belongings. Clothes were left in a pile in the corner, dolls abandoned on the floor, books left open. I was deliberately careless, confident in my ability to summon the Blue Fairy to my quarters. My sister came into my room shortly after I had climbed into my bunk. "This is a mess again!" she exclaimed. "What's gotten into you?" She seemed exasperated.

"The Blue Fairy will do it," I boasted.

"Don't be so sure about that," she answered. "The Blue Fairy may have better things to do than clean up your mess every night."

"You don't know that," I replied.

"I bloody well do," she snapped. "Who do you think the Blue Fairy is? Are you really that stupid?"

I looked at her in disbelief. It couldn't be possible, could it? Had she actually *seen* the Blue Fairy? "Did you see her?" I asked. "Do you know what she looks like?" I sat up in bed, "Tell me," I demanded, "tell me what she looks like."

"God, you're dumb," she answered. "I'm the Blue Fairy, all right? I did it for a joke. Are you ever gullible. Now clean up your own mess."

I have a Polaroid of us taken around that time. Sisters holding white-gloved hands. She is poised and polished, staring at the photographer with haughty impatience. And I, beside her, cardigan buttoned haphazardly, am gazing up at her. Willing myself to trust the appearance of her but remembering instead the stench and the screaming of The Monkey House.

The Wages of Sin

MYRA MILLERS IS HER NAME NOW. She married Tom Millers over on the tenth concession about five years ago. They grow potatoes, and some turnips and cauliflowers, but don't keep stock. He's too daft to keep anything much is what people say. No children neither. Likely too daft to figure that out, too. Or they keep apart. I don't want to think on that. Her next to him under the quilts and covers. His black fingernails touching her white skin. I wonder if she loosens her hair at night and lets it float soft about her face. Sinful thought.

When we was in school she used to wear plaits. They would swing beside her face when she moved. "Holy Jesus," I once said, "if you could let me hold one of those for just a minute, I promise I'll memorize the books in the Bible." I even started learning the Old Testament books—*Genesis, Exodus, Leviticus, Numbers, Deuteronomy*—to show I was serious. I tried to reach for one those plaits once when we was talking, but she jerked her head to the side like she was scared I was going to smack her. It made me sad to think she thought that. I stuck my hand in my pocket and didn't try again.

On Sundays, she tied on hair ribbons to match the dress she was wearing. She had a blue-and-white one and a yellow flowered one. They was the church dresses. During the week she wore plainer stuff to school like the others. "Holy Jesus," I said. "I bet the angels in heaven don't look as good as Myra on a Sunday." And that was true. There weren't a prettier girl in the county.

   I thought how she was pure as them little snowbells that came out each spring in my Ma's border. Tiny little perfect things poking out in the middle of all the winter muck and cold. Ma surely loved to see them and they were a wonder to behold. One Sunday, the preacher talked about God making Eve, and God said, *It is not good that the man should be alone; I will make him an help meet.* And so I prayed about it and it came to me that Myra was everything I needed in a wife and so I said, "Holy Jesus, if Myra marries me, I promise as how I'll set three layers aside and count out their eggs special and give the money to the missions." Three good layers means more than twenty eggs a week and I felt proud to be generous.

* * *

My Pa is always driving me hard. Between looking after the chickens and selling eggs all over the county, there wasn't time for much else. But Pa made sure we read our Bible together every night and, when the tent meetings came to town, we doubled up on chores so we could go. One summer, when the evangelists were all set up on the back of Derry's place, Pa and I set out walking. The cicadas were making that hot summer buzzing noise and I was glad to be wearing my best suit and to feel a few coins in the bottom of my pocket. Maybe there'd be a lemon drink afterwards, I thought, and a chance to visit friends. I might even get a glimpse of Myra if she was there.

   We were sitting on these plank benches at the back of the tent when I started feeling real hot, and I thought for sure that the preacher in the white suit was staring at me. He began weeping and got on his knees and called for the sinners to join him at the front and to repent of their sins. And I don't know what exactly happened, but my mouth started working and sounds was coming out and I couldn't stop it, and then I stood up and made my way to the front of the tent. And I knew that people were staring at me, but something was making me do it, and I cried some and got down on my knees, and promised to love Jesus with all my heart.

Afterwards the preacher said I was speaking in tongues and that the Holy Spirit had prompted me to come forward. Walking home, my Pa was mostly quiet ,but then he said, "Nellson, some things is sacred and now you made that pledge, you'd best keep it or endure the everlasting wrath of our God." That sure sobered me up. I heard Pa telling Ma about it when I was in bed and, for some reason, I kept hearing her ask him, "was it the heat?"

I woke up worried about God's everlasting wrath and tried to think what I could do to prove myself. And then it came to me that I could be like one of the apostles. But instead of being a fisherman, I was a poultry man. Same thing, we both provided food. The problem was how to be God's messenger and still do all of the chores I needed to do to keep up with the chickens? And I pored over my Bible, flipping pages and looking for something to tell me what to do. And then I found it: *For there shall arise false Christs, and false prophets, and shall shew great signs and wonders; insomuch that, if it were possible, they shall deceive the very elect* (Matt.24:24). And that just seemed the way of it. I would make signs and put them up around the county and warn people about the ways of sin and unfaithfulness.

I didn't talk to Pa about it. I just took some old boards and some red paint and started making signs. The first ones weren't too good. The words were messy and the paint all dripped down, looking like the letters was bleedin'. But I got better at it. Pa just looked at the pile of them in the egg delivery truck and never said a word. *For the wages of sin is death"* (Rom.6:23) and *And these shall go away into everlasting punishment* (Matt.25:46). I guess he thought as how I was doing what I needed. So, on those days when it was my turn for deliveries, I'd stop on the way home and nail up as many signs as I had ready.

* * *

God couldn't keep all my thoughts, no matter how hard I tried. Myra was always there. One day, between hanging pails of feed on the overhead trolley, I said, "Holy Jesus, if she just says anything to me I'll know that it's a sign and I'm supposed to do something." I thought hard about what I might do. Ask her to go for a walk maybe, down to the gorge or out to the pier? I liked to watch the sun set there sometimes, standing on the rocks of the old breakwater.

First thing after breakfast was the water pumping. I pumped forty-five gallons of water twice a day for the chickens. After setting their feed to rights, I checked the nests and filled the empty feed pails with the eggs I collected. A couple of hens started squawking and pecked my hand when I reached for the eggs. I had to push them away so they didn't go for my face. I put the pails of eggs back on the trolley and shoved them through to the feed room. When I was there, I took a minute to look at the backs of my hands. They were marked all over with scars, but today blood was dripping out of a couple of places where the skin got bit right off. "Holy Jesus," I said, "you bled for us, and I'm bleeding for these chickens." But then I got back to thinking about Myra. When I was doing my chores, it sure made things more pleasant. It couldn't be wrong to think of her so much, given how pure she was.

* * *

It's always my job to candle the eggs. I do this at night to see which eggs is fertilized and if the chick is growing. We mostly buy our chicks, but Pa thinks it's a good idea to hatch some of our own. He said as how it kept the birds happy. So he ties a ribbon to a nest to let me know which ones to leave alone when I'm collecting eggs. Then I go in at night and slip out the eggs and candle them to make sure they is growing right. I have to work real quick to make a pencil mark on them and make sure there's no cracks or rotten ones. And I have to be sure not to drop them neither. It's a pretty tricky business. But here's the thing: I like being out there at night. The sweet smell of fresh straw in the dark, and the warm close feeling you get when the birds is sleeping. Holding them warm eggs, even with bits of shit and straw stuck to them, it's a pretty good feeling. I like to hold them for a bit, and stroke the round end with my open hand and sometimes I close my eyes and think I'm holding onto something else. Maybe it's Myra's arm or one of her little tits. And that causes a stirring in my privates, and then I have to go to the privy and relieve myself, groaning when the seed comes out and asking Jesus to forgive me.

* * *

There was this big community supper planned and we was all donating food and then we was going to use the money to build an arena. The men were roasting a side of beef and the women were baking pies and cakes and after there was going to be a dance with some fiddlin'. And I thought as how I was above seventeen and she was near sixteen that it was all right for us to maybe start thinking about getting together. And so after church, I said to her, "Myra can I walk you to the supper next Saturday?"

And she turns this soft pretty pink and says to me, "Nells, that's a very nice offer but I'm going with my family. Maybe we could have a dance instead?"

And I took a step back and a good lung full of air, and I said, "Sure. A dance would be good," and I leave straightaway, feeling like my guts were boiling and my head was on fire.

* * *

The day of the supper, I was busy preparing the brooder house. Pa was out doing the deliveries and the cleaning fell to me.

We was expecting a delivery of baby chicks in the next week and it was time to get the room ready. I removed the litter and the feed troughs first, and then hosed and scrubbed at the walls and floor boards. When that was done, I sprayed the ceiling and walls with whitewash. It was full of pesticide to keep the bugs down. Last thing I had to do before the supper was paint the floor with creosote and furnace oil. Then I hurried to get ready and scrubbed myself as clean as I made them walls and floor. I combed my hair down flat with water and put on my Sunday clothes. Ma give me a cut lemon to squeeze on my hands.

We got there partway through the meal, but there was still lots of food and plenty of room to sit down. I looked up and down the tables searching for a glimpse of Myra and her family. I was eager for the dancing to start and was ready to jump up and go to her. "Holy Jesus," I whispered, "just let me have the first dance with her and I'll do whatever you ask for the rest of my life." I saw her finally, in her yellow dress, sitting with her brothers at the end of a row of tables. As soon as the music started, I was on my feet and walking toward her. She looked over at me and smiled when she saw me coming, but Tom Millers was closer than me and he got there first. I stood and watched while she got up and took his hand and walked to the dancing. She picked Tom. A sharp tightening across my chest squeezed the breath right out of me and made me stumble a bit. I took hold of a nearby table and went slowly back to my place to sit down. "Holy Jesus," I said, "I accept your sign. Thy will be done."

After we got home that night, I opened my Bible and began to read until finally I found words that gave me direction. *Whosoever looketh on a woman to lust after her hath committed adultery with her already in his heart* (Matt.5:28). And I realized that I was sinning in my heart with Myra and that I couldn't serve two masters. I couldn't love God and be lusting after Myra all the time. And so I gave up Myra, but the stirring inside my privates just got worse and I knew it was the devil tempting me.

* * *

Last night, when everyone was sleeping, I went for a long walk across the fields and over to the Millers' place. There was shovels and some tools just left lying in the grass and the woodpile was a mess with over-sized logs not split right. The wash line was flapping a little and I saw Tom's shirts on it waving their arms at me. At one end of the line was her clothes and I went to look. I leaned in to smell the soap on what must be a thin white slip or nightdress, all edged in lace. Beside it was a bunch of fine drawers. They had lace panels on them and didn't look like anything I'd ever seen before. Before I knew what it was doing, my hand reached out and took one, jamming it deep inside my jacket pocket. I felt it burn. Then I walked up close to the house and I looked in the parlour window and saw that the table was covered in an oilskin cloth with gears lubricating in grease on top, and some other thing spread out that needed a repair. "Cleanliness is next to godliness," is what Ma always said. She wouldn't be happy to see Myra's parlour. I got to nail up a sign for Tom to read, I thought. He and Myra don't come to church all that regular and they should.

So this afternoon I drove down the tenth and parked the truck and walked close so I could see that Tom was out working with the seeder. There's always a problem with Tom's machinery. He tries, but there's always something breaking or needing a new part. I walked back to my truck and pulled out a sign and a hammer and some nails. Quietly, without whistling or humming a hymn, I made my way back to the end of Tom's barn.

I climbed the pasture fence, and it took some doing, and leaned over to nail up my sign. I was still hammering when Tom came over. His face got all red when he saw what I was at.

"What the hell, Nells, what are you doing that for?" he shouted.

"Hey, Tom," I called out.

It was one of my nicer jobs. *If we confess our sins, he is faithful and just to forgive us sins, and to cleanse us from all unrighteousness* (1 John 1:9). I thought as how I wanted Myra to read it and start to come to church again.

"Nells, why in the goddamn hell are you nailing your bloody sign to my barn?"

"It's God's word, Tom," I answered simply. No point getting into an argument.

"Well take it the hell down, we don't want it."

"It's God's word, Tom," I answered, "be like tempting fate to take it down." And with that I hopped off the fence. I saw her then. She must've heard Tom shouting and she came outside and stood there on the porch. Her hair was pinned up tight and she had her hands on her hips. She saw me looking at her and brushed something off her front, and then fixed me a nice smile. I nodded at her and began to walk back to my truck. I heard him shouting after me, "You're crazier than a dog in heat, Nellson, you mind my words!"

When I got home, I went straight to the privy and I pulled out those white lace drawers and rubbed them against my privates until I was in agony. "Holy Jesus, help me," I called just before the release. I scrubbed away at my hands and arms with a stiff brush. I do this every night, but somehow my seed and the grit and grease has just settled into the cracks and pores of me.

A Love Story

THE TELEVISION SHOWED the ongoing protests. Signs stating, "Butchery" and "Government Allows Torture of Women" were carried by an aging crowd. A middle-aged spokeswoman with flaming red hair led the chanting. Passersby stopped momentarily to survey the scene and accept a leaflet. The media circled provocatively. Using the remote, she leaned forward in her chair and turned it off.

Bending to lace her black leather shoes, the woman whispered, "Hail Mary, full of grace." She pulled the laces tightly into a trim bow and continued, "The Lord is with thee." Having finished tying the second bow, she stood slowly erect. Smoothing her tweed skirt, she moved to the mirror and patted at her hair, tucking a strand behind her left ear. Reaching for her brown handbag, she moved to the pram and adjusted the light woolen blankets inside.

The babe was still asleep. Tentatively, she grasped the pram's handle with one hand, pulling it behind her and through the back door, which she held open with her foot. "It can't be too hard to make the butcher," she reasoned. "It's but three streets away." Stepping forward, she pulled the door closed behind her. Pushing the pram forward, her handbag looped over her arm, she made her way to the small garden gate and let herself out. The pram bounced gently up and down, its oversized springs and leather straps cushioning the uneven cobbles.

The babe slept on, not knowing that each of her mother's cautious footfalls corresponded with a sharp intake of breath. Unaware of the tightened clasp of fine white fingers on the pram's handle as they moved timidly forward. The young mother's gait was awkward as she laboriously swung her right leg to the side and then forward without bending the knee.

Her husband had wept when he saw the wound. His fingers lightly brushed the stubble of fine red that had once curled softly on the mound of her opening, tracing the line of swollen tissue that ran to her navel. "They saved the babe," she soothed, stroking the back of his head with her hand, "they did what was needful." But he wept against her sore place, his face pressed against the ragged, angry seam. She felt the ferocity of his grief and knew that their moments of intimacy would not now come easily.

Her mother had known what to do. She ripped a bed-sheet and wrapped her hips tightly with long cotton strips. The woman stood silent while her mother fastened the cotton together with secure knots. The gentleness of her mother's touch brought tears to her eyes. The pressure felt comforting to her, and although her first reluctant steps were still painful, the bonds provided some small security.

She remembered the room, its chill, the white tiles, and the feel of her bare feet in the stirrups. The nuns had held her down while the doctor and his assistant took her leg and pulled it sideways until something in her hip popped and she felt her insides ripping. She passed out from the pain. When she awoke, she saw that she was alone in the same strange white room, now splattered bright red. She could not move. A coarse sheet had been pulled up over her mouth to her nose. She tried to call out, but her mouth was filled with the cotton. She felt herself choking. "My babe," she thought, "where have they put my babe?"

Two of the nuns returned to her after a long while. The one closest to her smelled of starch and lavender and strong soap.

She was grim faced, but her hands were gentle. She washed the woman's face with cool water and moistened her lips with the corner of a wet towel. Neither of them spoke to her. The young thin one pushed on her stomach, and the woman cried out with the sudden searing. The older nun came close and shushed her softly. The doctor entered, unspeaking, but nodding to the small group who had followed him in. "She is ready now," he pronounced. Confused and terrified, the woman tried to struggle but discovered that she had been tightly strapped to the table. She screamed for her husband, roared his name, but the skinny nun pushed a white towel into her mouth. She felt herself choking, then dying, and the room went black around her.

The hospital had seemed like a luxury to them. Her husband was proud to have saved the money for the newest in medicine. When her labour had started, he called for a cab and they stood together on the curb. She was distraught at their parting and clung to him for too long while the nuns waited. His own waiting seemed interminable. He paced overnight in the murky green hallway, wringing his hands and kicking at bits of grit on the polished floor. He watched through the glass in the doors as the doctor came down the stairs and approached him with news of his daughter. Days later, he would remember the fine spray of blood on the doctor's eyeglasses.

The babe was three months old now, and she was going to bathe her without assistance. The woman concentrated on her preparations, limping while she carried the towels and talc into the kitchen. The tiny tub was placed on the table, and her mother filled it with warm water. Carefully, she bent down, stripped off the baby's wet nightgown and pulled away the diaper. Clasping the infant to her chest, she kissed her small head and carried her to the tub. Her mother watched from a chair in the corner. "Slowly, love," she called. "There's no hurry."

Unsteadily, the woman sat the child in the warm water and supported her back and neck with her left hand. Gently, she splashed some water and began to softly soap her, her fingers carefully finding the small folds of skin. The mother watched intently, perched on the edge of the wooden chair, ready to leap up if needed.

It was time, the mother knew, for her daughter to try. She had heard the other savage stories by now. The fancy doctors were clear that those with small feet had small openings, and needed "a procedure" to help the babies come out. Child's feet are what her daughter had, slim little child's feet. That was the problem. The long, angry scar was bad enough, but the circles under her eyes and the shaking hands were a worry. The girl's nerves were gone and, with them, her spark.

The young woman was exhausted by the time the babe was dried, dressed, fed, and once again asleep in her pram. The laundry needed attention and there was nothing prepared for her husband's meal. Her mother offered to start the laundry and scrape potatoes and carrots if she went to the butcher for a pound of beef. Holding onto the pram would steady her, her mother reasoned, and the air would be good for the babe.

Each step felt as though broken glass were rubbing at her insides. Sharp pains tore at her thighs and up inside her. Perspiring from the effort, she stopped after one block to catch her breath and wipe at her brow with a handkerchief. The babe slept sweetly. Steadying herself, she resumed. A soft whimper of pain escaped when she jarred her right leg on a raised cobble, sickening her stomach.

The exchange at the butcher's was dream-like. "A pound of stew beef," she asked, and was handed the paper-wrapped parcel. It felt cold in her hand, and heavy. She paid for her modest purchase and deliberated risking the walk to the bakery. The bakery was across the road and down a bit. Her husband would love a crusty loaf, she knew. And so she began to make her way. It was then that the sensation of warmth appeared on top of the grinding glass and she felt a trickle making its way down the inside of her thigh. She looked down in horror, but could not see what it was she felt. Then the faint odour wafted up and she froze, frightened that another step would release more down her legs and onto the roadway. Scarlet, she turned the pram around sharply and headed back. As she stepped toward home, more trickled its way down her stockings until she could see the evidence beneath her skirt hem, the dripping running into her shoes.

The smell of the stew greeted him when he opened the door. It was a good sign. His mother-in-law must still be here, he thought. He couldn't think how they would manage without her daily visits. Stepping into the kitchen, he saw that the table was nicely set for two. Walking to the pram, he stopped to watch his daughter sleeping and smiled at her. "You're as fine as a baby angel," he said to her. "Though you caused your ma' some trouble." He called out for his wife. She appeared at the top of the stairs, wearing a Sunday dress.

"You're home," she greeted him, "and I've stew ready."

He grinned back at her, delighted. This was a first. She began to step down the stairs, and he saw the effort it still was. He moved forward and climbed the bottom steps quickly to grab hold of her and carry her down. She put her arms around his neck and rested her head on his shoulder. He lifted her gently and carried her to the kitchen chairs. "Sit," he said, "let me fill the bowls."

Their nighttime routine had become established. He carried the child up first, and then he carried up his wife. He had taken to sleeping on a spare cot in their room. When they had shared the bed his movements had made her twinge with pain. It was only until she healed, he reasoned, and then all would return to rights. But time had passed and there was little sign of healing. "Some women take to having babies and some women don't," is what the men at work had said.

She knew that it was his love for her that kept them apart. Sometimes before turning in at night, his fingers would draw gentle trails on her neck, slipping down inside her nightdress and continuing their soft patterning. She would turn towards him, willing her body to respond to his touch and the aching of desire. She would press herself to him, massaging his back with her hands and burying her face in his chest. Prying himself away, he would whisper, "Not now, love, mind yourself."

Once or twice he allowed her to reach for him and called her a "bold thing" while she rubbed him into a frenzy. But when the deed was done and he was spent, they both felt cheated. His friends told him to try entering her from behind. There was no damage there, they reasoned. He had been shy to ask her and worried that it were a sin, but their longing for intimacy was such that they agreed to try. She undid her clothing quickly and stood before him with only the bandages swathed tightly around her hips. He was frightened by the thinness of her, shocked to see the bones in her back and ribs raised beneath the skin. Carefully, he ran his hands down her spine and began to strip the bandages, slowly unwinding them and discarding them onto the floor. She went to the end of the bed. Bracing herself against the footboard, she bent forward slightly and waited for him. He stepped out of his clothes quickly and pushed against her. His hands reached around and gently cupped her small breasts. He kissed the back of her neck and her shoulders and whispered words of love. But the thrusting filled her with pain. He felt her wince, and a tiny moan escaped from her. "Don't stop," she whispered, but he could not continue.

On the doctor's orders, the dispensary gave her tablets to try, but they did not take away the cut glass sensation or the throbbing. He prescribed exercises to strengthen her right leg, but it continued lame. And then a new doctor set up a practice across the common. Her mother told her that it was "worth trying somebody new," and so she made an appointment. She described her troubles to him, and he asked to examine her. The nurse came in to help her undress and covered her with a sheet on the table. He did not open her legs or put them in stirrups. He pressed gently on her hips and pubis and said that he was done. When she was dressed again and once more seated in his office, he told her that she needed to have some x-rays, and he wrote out an order for them. "Where did you have the child?" he asked.

When she told him, he grimaced, but quickly regained his composure. "Well, then, let's have these done elsewhere." He held the door open for her when she left and patted her gently on her shoulder when she passed through.

Her mother went with her for the second doctor's appointment. "It was not a Caesarian-section you had," said the doctor. "It was a procedure that some practice to encourage more children.* They have cut your pelvic bone. The tendons and muscles that work your right leg have also been severed, and they will not mend. I have seen others, also from that place, who have had the same procedure. You have been badly damaged, and the pain must be fierce."

She was so relieved to hear it that she wept.

"What is to be done?" her husband asked when she returned home. "Is there nothing to be done?"

On Easter Sunday, they set out for Mass. The woman was slow, and the man carried their small daughter. Church bells were pealing across the town, and the woman listened for the distinct bells of the Annunciation that were so familiar to her. They stopped to dip their fingers into the holy water and to cross themselves when they entered. The woman touched her hat to ensure that it was on straight. The church was filled with fresh spring flowers, and the Lenten clothes that had draped the statuary in mourning had been removed. They stopped at a pew to genuflect before sliding in. The woman did this awkwardly, her right leg stretched out straight, while she knelt partway down with her left knee. She held on to the side of the pew, but then could not cross herself. She bowed her head and hoped that would suffice. Her husband reached out to steady her.

Once seated, she reached for his hand and smiled at him. "I will be well," she thought, "I must be well." After Mass, they lined up with others to receive a blessing from the priest. He placed his hand on their daughter's forehead and made the sign of the cross with his thumb. "How old is she now?" he asked.

"Nineteen months, next week," replied the proud father.

"It will be time, then, for another," intoned the priest, looking pointedly at the woman. She flushed red and bowed her head, disgraced. They made their way down the front stairs, the woman clinging to her husband's arm for support.

"Feck it" said her husband. "The old fecker doesn't know what he's about."

The new doctor was dedicated in his efforts to help. He prescribed padded insoles for her shoes, heavy pads for her incontinence, and a walking stick for support. An associate of his suggested a pelvic girdle, and the husband had one fashioned by a shoemaker. The leather was thick and, when worn over her undergarments, allowed her to finally discard the cotton strips she had continued to use to bind herself. Under this doctor's care, she was gradually able to assume the responsibility for the shopping and housework and cooking and laundry. It took her longer to do these things, but she was determined to resume the routines that had once made her so happy.

The husband remained kind and gentle. On Friday nights, he joined his mates at the pub while she stayed home with the child. This was a new routine. At first he came home after one pint, but after several months, his nights out lengthened. She waited up for him, dozing in the stuffed chair. He would come in and nuzzle her neck affectionately before carrying her up the stairs to their room. She placed her arms about his neck happily and was glad to see him feeling light-hearted.

On Tuesdays and Thursdays, she walked to the high street to shop. Afterwards, she went to the Annunciation to light two candles. The first candle was always for her family, and the second candle was for herself. At first, she prayed for healing, but when the pain did not cease, she found herself praying for the strength to bear it. Finally, when the pain had emptied her, she began to pray for the courage to do what was needed.

After a long while, when the husband returned from the pub, there was a trace lingering of perfume or flowered shampoo. The woman said nothing, but wrapped her arms about him as usual and let him lift her up the stairs. Then one Friday night, he did not nuzzle her when he came in, stammering instead that he was feeling a bit "weak in the knees." He did not look at her when he said this, but busied himself picking up discarded toys.

His wife bit her lip as if attacked by another of her pains. Her eyes stung as she tried to blink away the suddenness of the change. "Let's to bed then," she finally said, and she moved to the staircase on her own. He stood watching, not able to draw close. "I will always love you," she said, "no matter."

And this, then, became a newer routine. She would struggle to cope with her chores, and then she would greet him warmly at the end of his day, wearing a fresh dress, with a hearty dinner ready. He, in turn, would hold his daughter on his lap and play with her on the floor, faithfully fulfilling his responsibilities on all nights but the one. On Friday nights, he would return home when the pub shut and sleep downstairs on the two-seater.

The unrelenting torment was now all too familiar. The simple mention of her pain made the man sad and sometimes angry. He could not reconcile the look of her with the young slip of a girl who had teased and bewitched him only three years before. Unbidden, his mind often conjured a picture of her dancing with a blue summer dress and black leather slippers, hopping and kicking out the steps, and then twirling lightly in front of him, laughing when the music stopped. The memory no longer seemed possible. He closed his eyes, replaying her like a film or a fairytale: his young bride skipping away from him in her wedding dress, teasing him to chase after her for want of a dance and a kiss. Remembering the feel of her softness when they first made bold to explore each other in the darkness, and the gentle caress of her hand on his chest when they lay still together afterwards. The tantalizing surprise of her. The making of their child when she had mounted him, arching her back and crying out at his pleasure, bending her head down to his and draping him with her hair.

Then one Sunday, at breakfast, she said, "I think you should go." The sound of it shocked them both. "The priest will not fault you," she continued, "for leaving me. I can be your wife in name only."

He was silent, absorbing her words and what they suggested. "How will you manage?" he finally asked.

"My da' will take me back. I have spoken with them. They know it is right."

The man began to sob, low guttural cries wrenched from deep inside. She went to him and held his head to her stomach, patting his shoulders and comforting him. And although he clung to her while he wept, he did not argue.

When the first wave of his grief was spent, she stepped away and he saw that she had packed a small suitcase for him that stood ready by the door. He walked over to it and felt its heft, and he was once more overcome by emotion. She could not have lifted this herself, he knew. And he realized that she must have filled it by making many trips. It was an act of love that had driven her. And he thought of the money they had carefully saved when she was pregnant. Both of them trying to do everything right and finding instead, that life had dealt them a cruel blow. And their daughter was growing up despite them and would never understand how much it hurt him to look at her and know that, despite the joy of her, her very entry to the world had ruined his happiness.

And so he picked up the suitcase and walked out the door. He left believing that they could not continue as they were. And the woman watched him leave.

*Symphysiotomy is the name of a surgical procedure performed on some Catholic women in Ireland from the late1940s to the mid-1960s. The practice involved widening the pelvis through the division of the pubic symphysis. This was often done without the prior knowledge, or consent, of the women. The procedure was frequently performed using force and crude instruments, and without anesthetic or medication for pain. The majority of women were left compromised by trauma, chronic pain, lameness, and incontinence.

A Hawk in Winter

JIM MAY LOOK LIKE A GILHAM, but he acts like Ellie's no-good brother. *A tall drink of water* is what Ellie always said. *As welcome anywhere as a tall drink of water.* Trouble is, water don't always quench a deep thirst. Oh, her brother could spin a tale and charm anyone in a skirt, but he had no sticking power. Jim's just the same. Time was, I thought Gwen would be the making of him. They'd have babies and he'd settle into the routine of things. But that weren't how it worked out.

I ran into Larmar at the dump this morning. "Saw Gwen at the IGA," he said, "looked good for a divorcée."

"Back is she?" I checked. "Visiting?" What in the hell would he know about it?

"Nope, said she was looking for work. Asked me if I knew anything."

Larmar's a dairy man. Known him all my life. He's a scrawny sonofabitch and too goddamn cheap to drink any of the cream he collects in those big vats of his. I took my time answering. There was a jumpy feeling in my gut. "Well," I said, "guess I better be off. Keep your pecker up." I climbed into my old Ford and pulled out of the parking lot, getting the hell away as fast as I could.

Holy shit, I thought. Like there weren't enough trouble lately. Talk was Jim wasn't paying his men; kept stalling their cheques. That was the sort of thing you couldn't keep quiet in a small place. Jim's my eldest and he's one holy pain in the arse.

Maude wanted some attention when I got home. She's always nuzzling. I got her for Ellie. But Ellie went to hospital soon after. I took Maude out one night when she was still a pup, and a big hawk came right down outta nowhere an' tried to snatch her. I bent over to protect her, and she jumped into my arms and piddled all down the front a my shirt. Figure it was a red-tail—four foot wingspan and bold as brass. Thing is, when the hospital called in the morning, I was ready. The hawk was an omen.

"It would seem Gwen's back," I said to Maude. "Don't know what she expects." I rinsed a fancy cup under the tap. One of Ellie's favourites. "Maybe she'll straighten him out now she's back. Course, he'd never have been in this mess if she'd stayed." I reached over to the electric stove and turned on the burner.

"Guess that's not fair now, is it?" I asked, scratching at her head while she rubbed against my leg. "I always liked her, ya' know. Better than my own son most days."

I sat myself down at the breakfast table. The window still had Ellie's curtains. Fuzzy with dust. Two years now since the cancer took her and a year since Gwen showed up wearing nothing but her nightie. Standing on the porch crying when I opened the door. She'd taken a beating and was all over cut and bloody. I picked her up and carried her through to my bedroom and tucked her into the warm bed. Later, when she was sleeping, I drove to Jim's and dragged him outside. It grieved me to have at my own flesh and blood, but it was a lesson long overdue. It weren't the first time he got drunked up and hurt her, but it was sure as hell going to be the last. I left the smarmy bastard bleeding in the dirt, his nose and jaw likely broke, and went inside to get her clothes. Packed her off in the morning. Sent her with Jim's car and all the cash I had in my freezer.

While I was sitting with my coffee gettin' cold, I watched a few flakes a snow drifting down, lacing things with white. And then a hawk flew by, its gold markings clear against tawny feathers, legs outstretched. Likely hunting for a field mouse. I watched the hawk until it was out of sight. Then the phone rang.

"Ian," I heard, "it's me. I'm home."

I stood back a bit, steadying myself, "Well now, what about that?" I replied.

"I'd like to see you. Can I come?"

"Well, sure," I answered. "I'm always glad to see a pretty girl."

"Now?"

"Why sure. Sure. That would be fine." After hanging up the phone, I messed about the kitchen for a bit, filling the kettle, opening the fridge and shutting it. I looked in the mirror on the back of the door and smoothed my hair down. Still looked okay for an old bugger, I thought. Bit on the weathered side, but built hard and tight. I fingered my old red-and-black jack-shirt, trying to decide if I should put it on. I heard a car in the lane. It was Gwen. I went outside. *Lithe*, I thought, she is what Ellie called *lithe*.

She came rushing forward to hug me. She smelled good and just tucked herself in against my chest. Her head filling the hollow under my chin, pressing against my throat. Her hair was different, cut short.

"Why, hello, stranger. How ya' been?" I asked.

"Oh, Ian, I'm glad to be home. How are you? How's Maude?" Linking her arm in mine, she squeezed it tight, holding me trapped for a minute, and then ran inside to greet Maude. When she bent down to pat the dog, I had a clear view of her little tits and a fancy brassiere. Been a while since I seen one a' them up close. And never like that. Lord almighty.

"It's good to be back." She looked up at me, smiling, when I followed her into the room. Still looked young. Twenty-two when she and Jim were married. Twenty-four when she left. I could still see her freckles. Faded a bit. God, she was the cutest little thing when he first brought her around. The two of them looking all moonstruck. Couldn't keep their hands off each other. Ellie and me, we knew what that was about.

"You need some sun," I said. "You look pale."

"I'm fine. There's nothing wrong with me."

"Would you like something to eat?"

"Yes, I'm starved. Let me do." She began moving around the kitchen, pulling out plates and bread and cheese, setting the table, wiping down the counter. She was wearing a flowered skirt, and there were flashes of skin showing between her top and belt as she reached for things. I looked away most times.

"C'mon," she said, looking all happy. "Sit. It's ready." We sat down and looked out the window at the snow falling.

"I thought about you," Gwen said. "A lot."

What'n the hell, I thought, sucking in a bit of air. I'm twice her age. Truth is, though, I can still hold my own. I got the largest sheep farm in the township and can still grip and sheer them in record time. I shame younger fellas at the fair each year who ain't got my strength or touch. Reckon I can likely manage some of them other things too. Everything's still in working order.

"Well then," I said, feeling my neck and face colouring hot. "Jim know you're here?"

"No. Not yet. I want to be home, Ian. I want to be here. But not with Jim. I can't do that again." She looked a little wobbly, like one of my new lambs finding its legs and trying to feed for the first time. Before the colostrum takes and they gets all bouncy. It hit me.

"He needs you, Gwen. He messed up all right, but he needs you."

"If he was just more like you...." Gwen's voice wavered. I looked for tears but saw only her stubborn streak setting in. Her chin tipped up. Lips held tight.

I ate my cheese sandwich. "You know, Gwen, things weren't always easy for Ellie and me. We had to work at it. Jim's having a tough time with the company. People don't pay their bills. And you know he's no good with money."

"What do you mean?"

"Why someone, say Calvin Cawker, builds a brand new house. Red brick over on the town-line, and he gets Jim to do the ducts. And then he says he don't like where the vents are and so he's not gonna' pay. Jim's out time and materials. I saw Calvin the other day, and I gave him what for and all he said was that if Jim wanted money, he could whistle fur it."

"I know, Calvin. What got into him?"

"Ah, he's always been a self-important little shit. Thinks he knows everything."

Gwen placed her hand on mine. The lanolin keeps mine soft, but hers weren't so rough neither. Felt pretty good. Been a long time since someone touched me.

"Are you okay?"

I looked down and studied the vinyl floor tiles—black and white checkerboard. I wasn't for looking at her just then. Slowly, I pulled my hand out from underneath. "Well, I never have been more broke, that's for sure. Had to help Jim out with a bill or two. Don't always do so well on my own. I killed one of Ellie's climbers last spring. Didn't prune it right. Just hacked it."

"I needed some time." She looked at me intently for a minute, and then said, "I miss Ellie too, you know."

"Yep," I nodded. "I know."

I watched her stroking her skirt tight against her legs. I picked up a table knife and ran my nail along the serrated edge, back and forth.

"Well, now, what are your plans?" I asked. My voice sounded unnatural. I felt hot, and my head was starting to pound. I looked out the window again.

"I'm not sure. Look for work, I guess. I'm staying at Gran's for now."

"Heard you was settled in the city."

"It didn't work out." Gwen stood up and began to pace.

"Tell me," I said softly. "What happened?" But I figured I already knew. I pictured her in another place. Pictured her lifting off that nightgown and peeling it away from her body. Standing there, waiting.

Gwen let out a small breath. She came back to the table and sat at the far end. "I needed to come home. I needed to see how things stood between us."

I was chewing my lip. Hard at it. "Gwen," I began, "I'm starting to get older now and I see things. I been watching this pair of hawks. They nest in the elm at the edge of that field. Those birds perch hunt. They sit until they spot something they want, and then they go for it. Just fly down and grab. No dilly-dallying."

Gwen nodded, and then in a choky voice, she said, "I thought you'd be glad I came back."

I pretended I didn't get her meaning. Just looked at the frayed place mat in front of me and said, "Not like this. Jim's not gonna' change. He's pissed away every cent he ever had and lots that weren't his, besides. You gotta' grab your happiness, Gwen."

"What are you saying?"

"If Ellie were here, she'd want you to be happy," I said.

I stood up and went to her and bent down for a quick goodbye. I rubbed the side of my cheek in her hair. "You take care now." And then I reached for my jack-shirt and went outside.

I walked hard across the field and down into the woods, scanning the sky and the trees. I remembered having watched that hawk with its mate, arching in mid-air last spring, talons locked together, cart-wheeling and tumbling. And now I was remembering what it was to clutch at love while spiralling slowly to the ground.

Oliver Hambley

OLIVER HAMBLEY WAS AS WELL KNOWN for his hospitality as he was for his good nature. Word was that he'd not only give you the shirt right off his back, but he'd thank you for the privilege. It wasn't always that way though. Dulcie set him to rights. She was the real making of him, folks said. He was always a likeable fellow. Given a bit to self-indulgence though. The truth is he had a history of some serious drinking. It started when he was young and too poor to do much else. He carried into the world besides, his personal shame like an open wound just festering. His father held the family purse strings, and although Oliver worked a man's job, he was never given a man's wages for his labours. When he wanted money, he had to say, "If you please," and "if you don't mind," and go begging of his own father for what was, most would rightly say, his share.

But Jack Hambley was as mean as he was miserly, and so Oliver would thumb a ride to town without a coin in his pocket. Those who felt sorry for him would stand him a drink, and soon Oliver would forget the meanness at home and begin to sing for his whiskey, entertaining the room with favourite songs and old hymns. He had the gift of his mother's music although, in fact, not many people could actually remember having heard Mary McCullough's voice. She had been tethered to the farm for so long, and had grown so stout with childbearing and chores, that it was hard to reconcile the spent and weathered woman with the dark-haired, spirited thing who had once sung in the Methodist choir. Jack Hambley had been a promising young man. He had cleaned up nicely and had had big ideas. People thought that she had fallen in love with his fool notions as much as she had with his good looks and company manners. His money-making schemes gradually took their toll on her however and she was often left alone, swollen with child, to cope with another of his schemes.

Mary had been left so often that each time her neighbours wondered if this would be the last time she would wait for him. But she always waited. And Jack would return, some months hence, tail between his legs, with stories of how close he had come to greatness and how some crook had swindled him out of *his* chance. And then he would set to around the farm, fixing fences and building sheds in a flurry of activity that would last eight or ten months. After a while, good suit on and cardboard suitcase in hand, he would be sighted again, slinking off in search of dreams.

Jack's wanderings were legendary, and the tales about him were a source of local lore. The winter of 1924 changed the fortunes of both Jack and the township. Jack returned from a trip to the city with something he called "purifying tablets." Instead of pumping water from the well for the stock, he informed people, you could divert water from the river for the animals and wouldn't need to worry about whatever was upstream. Every day, you would just toss a tablet into the watercourse and the chemicals would make it safe for drinking. Jack had bought several boxes of these tablets from a *real* scientist, he said, and was willing to sell them to his neighbours for a small profit.

Now the thing about Westone was that in the late summer there was sometimes a drought that dried up the wells for a time and made drinking water scarce. The Mercy River was sluggish and muddy, and although it crossed many of the farms, farmers kept their animals away because the mill upstream made the water smell. But that summer, after several weeks without rain, the farmers made their way to Hambley's to purchase a paper packet filled with the inch-round, sulphur-smelling pills.

Delighted to finally come into his own as a forward-thinking man, Jack counted his growing receipts with excitement. But then the wells began to dry up entirely and, satisfied that the animals had not suffered, Jack extended the merits of his pills and encouraged folks to use river water for household use as well, boasting that the pills were one hundred percent guaranteed.

When he heard about the latest claim, Doc Beacock drove to Hambley's and raised the devil, throwing the remaining pills out the front door with, "For shame, Hambley, tellin' lies to get people sick." And so the drought that year came to be associated with Hambley's shame, and Jack was blamed, with some merit, for the grip, the diarrhoea, and all manner of intestinal disorders that spread through the country that summer.

It was the arrival of his son, Oliver, that left people whispering about the ill-advised effects of the pill. Oliver was born with a clubfoot, and he dragged his left leg around like a heavy weight. Jack hated the boy and treated him cruelly, venting the frustrations of his own misspent energies on the deformity. Fortune had gifted Oliver with some grace however, and Oliver's chance blessing was his mother's ear for music and a strong, rich voice that could fill the corners of a room with its power.

When he was home, Jack ruled the household with an iron fist, and with his belt always at the ready. His three eldest sons considered themselves lucky to enlist, and left the farm to meet the recruiting agent at their first chance. By the time Oliver was seventeen, he was left as the only farm help, cumbersome and hated by his father as he was. But his lovely voice was deep and sonorous, coursing through the mire of chores and unhappiness with the songs of his ancestors, the radio, and the Psalmist in equal measure. A couple of years passed in this way.

Jack was only in his forties when Oliver found him in the field with his arm ripped off by the threshing machine. The belt was still running and the engine was hot to the touch. Oliver sat in the field and held his father's head, the loss more real perhaps than the single letter from England that had marked the irrevocable departure of his brothers. He wailed so loudly that his mother finally heard him from the summer kitchen. Oliver sat in the bloody dirt and keened, swatting people away until the doctor arrived and began his morbid inventory. Mary suspended what she felt of grief and moved through the rituals of burying: readying the front room, turning out the pantry, loosening the hinges on the parlour door, and pressing their best clothes.

She and Oliver set to their chores with little emotion, and greeted the sorry-sayers with calm and resignation. Oliver was standing with a group of men outside the house after the burial lunch when he noticed his cousin, Dulcie, watching him.

"Hullo, Dulcie," he called out, "are you well?"

"As well as you, no doubt," she answered, approaching him closely and then stopping a few feet from him, "and better perhaps."

One of the men chuckled at her saucy tone, but the others continued talking, excluding Oliver for the moment, and freeing him to accept the customary condolences and sympathies.

"Well," said Oliver, moving towards her.

"Well," said the pert girl, "you'll be needing to marry now. I'm your cousin and as good as you're likely to get. Think about it." And just as abruptly she turned and walked back across the yard and towards the house.

Oliver watched her, slack-mouthed. It was a bold thing she'd done. He coloured deeply just watching the sway of her as she moved up the porch steps and in through the front door. A couple of weeks later, he worked it into a conversation with his mother. "Isn't Dulcie about marrying age?" was the shape of his enquiry.

"And why would you be askin'?" his mother snapped, staring at him suddenly, reading his face. The room grew silent with the intensity of their exchange. Both of them needing to know.

"I just wondered, is all," said Oliver, "if another pair of hands around here might be a help."

"Well, if it's marrying you're thinkin' of," said Mary, "she's as likely as the rest, I suppose."

"But what do you think?" persisted Oliver. "Would you be glad of the company?"

"It's not me that'll be sharing a bed with her, Oliver. You choose. But choose well. Your lot will be the more bitter if you choose wrong." And Mary looked down at the bowl of potatoes she was peeling and recommenced her work.

Oliver chewed on her words for a while and finally took them as a sort of permission. Several nights later, fortified by drink, and encouraged by a crew of flat-footed, left-behind friends, he exited the Dominion Hotel and made his way to his cousin's house, where he was welcomed by his Uncle James. Oliver stammered out the purpose of his call, and his Uncle called Dulcie to the room.

Dulcie seemed not unprepared for his arrival, and linked her arm in his as they moved together to the car. "I knew that you would come for me, you know," she began by way of greeting.

"Well, that I have," agreed Oliver.

And the two of them settled the business between them in a tiny gore of land adjacent to the Mercy River, the long grass wet with dew, and the pair of them damp and rumpled from their time there. For Oliver and Mary and Dulcie, the time following the small wedding was a respite in their unhappy struggles, and they worked for the war effort with confidence and energy. Dulcie slipped into their daily routines easily and made a quiet place for herself. They were often amused by her cheerful approach and delighted by her thrift. Even Mary could be heard humming now and then while she went about her work. And so, for a time, Oliver felt that he should be a happy man, and Mary congratulated herself on having the good fortune to claim at least one remaining son and a biddable daughter-in-law.

Despite their losses and the changes that were happening, the farming community in Westone, for the most part, were surviving the war. Many of the young women had left to do work in the city or to join the female teams of roving farm help. Oliver had never felt the shame of his clubfoot more dearly. He worked like two men during this time, aware that, although his family was missing three sons, he, Oliver, was not seen to have suffered enough. His marrying had been viewed as selfish when so many young men were overseas. There was many a snide comment made in town, burning him deeply.

Most nights, they ate their supper listening to the news bulletins on the radio. One evening, when the news was particularly glum, Dulcie murmured something about wishing she could do more. And that comment, sharp on the heels of something he heard in town, seared Oliver. "No one's stopping you," he yelled at her in a sudden flare of temper. "I'll help you go!" Mary tried to intervene, but Oliver limped out of the house to the barn where he kept a bottle for just such occasions. Dulcie gathered her things together quickly.

"He didna' mean it, Dulcie," Mary repeated. "Stay and work things out in the morning."

But Dulcie kissed her goodbye and set out walking for her father's farm. She sent a postcard from the Women's Christian Temperance Union a couple of weeks later that said she had met up with Gracie Hawks and Helen Hodgins and that the three of them were working together. Her loss, coupled with the strangeness of life's turns, caused Oliver to throw the card in the stove and return to the barn where he now kept a good supply of comfort. Mary wept into her apron.

This continued for a month. Mary crying and Oliver drinking. And then James' old black Dodge crept up the lane and parked at the house. James found Oliver in the barn, a drink in him as usual, and began with, "It's a good whipping you need. Drinking the day away and your wife from home doing a man's job."

Oliver had the good sense to stay quiet and hear his uncle out.

"Now this is what you're going to do," continued James. "You're going to drive to Toronto and you're not going to show your face around here until Dulcie comes back with you." James turned to head back to his car, but stopped himself and looked at Oliver again. "And you're going to lay off the booze and act like a man. And if you don't, it's me you'll answer to. Do ya' hear?"

The next day, chores done, cash money in his pocket, Oliver left. He had to stop several times to ask the way. The traffic was unfamiliar and frightened him, and he found himself wondering at all of the activity. He located the Women's Christian Temperance Union and parked his car on a street nearby. He stood outside on the sidewalk, waiting for the girls to come back from work. Dulcie saw him first, and came over directly.

"Is everyone well at home?" she asked. "How's Mary?"

"We're well enough. Thank you. Dulcie, that's not why I'm come."

"Then why did you come?"

"To bring you back."

"Well, you're wasting your time if that's all you have to say."

"Can we go somewhere?" asked Oliver, looking pointedly at Helen and Gracie, who were watching the exchange closely.

"No, Oliver. Not tonight. It's late and I'm tired. Tomorrow."

"Dulcie, I got nowhere to go."

"The Porter will tell you where. Meet me here in the morning. At eight." And Dulcie turned and went to Gracie and Helen, and the three of them stepped inside the building.

Oliver found the hotel the Porter directed him to, and he took a room for two nights, deciding that things didn't look hopeful. He slept only a little. The walls were thin, and he was aware of unfamiliar city sounds that echoed in the small bare box of a room. He stood in the queue for the bathroom the next morning and tidied himself up before leaving to meet Dulcie.

He concentrated so intensely on noting landmarks and finding his way that he gave no thought as to what it was he would actually say to her. Pleased with himself for arriving early, Oliver stood outside the front door at the Women's Christian Temperance Union and whistled a low tune, feeling, generally, rather in good form.

They spent an awkward day together, not knowing how to incorporate their past intimacy into this new setting. They walked the streets, strolled in a public garden, and looked at the lakefront. Oliver insisted on a streetcar ride. Dulcie treated him politely and smiled indulgently, but moved away when he brushed up against her or stood too close. In the midst of a busy green lawn, she pointed out the Metropolitan United Church where she and the girls had been attending Sunday services. Oliver was amazed by its very size and whiteness, and kept asking who had paid for it all.

They ate in a diner that Dulcie knew. "One that didn't cost too much." After they had ordered, Oliver got to the business at hand.

"I'd like you to come home," he began. "Mary and your father miss you terrible." Oliver looked down at his hands while he spoke, studying the thickened, discoloured fingernail that he had hit with a hammer the previous week.

"Why would I leave my friends to come home and be miserable?" she replied.

Oliver put his hands on his knees and looked at the table carefully before responding, "Because it's your place."

"And what would I tell the girls?" Dulcie stared at Oliver defiantly, trying to catch his eyes with her own. Daring him to look at her.

"That you're needed at home," stated Oliver simply.

"That's not true," she argued.

"It is so!" Oliver answered sharply. He looked at her then,

hurt afresh by her pretending not to know. Wondering what she was about.

"Oliver," she began, "you're half out of your mind with drink most of the time. What would you care?"

Oliver's mouth gaped open at this fresh attack, and he shaped his lips a couple of times, trying to form a response. The waitress interrupted by delivering the cutlery and clattering it down on the table. And because they were both young, and both unaccustomed to such negotiations, they left off talking and ate their lunch.

Walking back to the Hall, Dulcie agreed to let Oliver come to church with her in the morning. Oliver wanted to see the inside of the building that had so impressed him. Dulcie wanted to be kind to Oliver, but she was not prepared to set aside her new routines for him. Church had become a part of her new life, and if he wanted to see her on Sunday, then he must come with her to church.

In the morning, after pleasantries had been awkwardly exchanged, they set off with Gracie and Helen to the Metropolitan United Church. As they drew closer, Oliver saw that the crowd was well dressed and that most of the men were in uniform. He hesitated, feeling self-conscious, and wondered if he should continue. As he stood still on the sidewalk, the carillon began to ring. Oliver had never heard such a joyful sound in his life.

The girls, mistaking his stance, assumed that he was simply listening to the bells. "There are twenty-three," said Gracie.

"And they're inscribed," added Helen, "*May the spirit of the Lord reach the heart of everyone where the sound of these bells is heard.*"

"Mr. Massey gave them in memory of his wife," finished Gracie.

Despite Oliver's self-consciousness, he allowed himself to be guided by Helen into the church. The four of them slipped into a pew near the middle of the sanctuary. Oliver was in awe of the bells and the vaulted ceiling and the windows and the overall beauty of the place, and he stared at his surroundings until the organ sounded and the congregation stood to sing:

Praise to the Lord, the Almighty, the King of creation;
O my soul, praise him, for he is thy health and salvation;
All ye who hear, brothers and sisters draw near,
Praise him in glad adoration.

Oliver listened to the magnificent organ intently for a moment, and then he began to sing along: his voice soaring in the cavernous space. People glanced at him, discreetly at first, but then more openly, wanting to identify the person who sang with such love and such power. Oliver was oblivious to the attention, and he continued to sing without restraint. Dulcie edged toward him and saw that his face was wet with tears. Oliver felt her move close to his side, and he looked at her tenderly. Still singing, he reached for her hand and pressed it tightly against his heart.

Blue Eyes

THE SUN SEEMED SUBDUED and was barely visible behind the cloudy haze. The seals were on a rock, a half mile or so from shore. Black heads bobbed in the water, and now and again there was a splash as one of them dove beneath the surface. There was a steady, quiet languor to the day. The seals and the ocean and the terns drifted at leisure. Birdcalls and the soft clattering of shifting stones and crashing waves sounded.

In the near distance, to my right, was a large sandy outcrop. I was lying on the beach in a small cove, accessible only at low tide. Exhausted from the long commute, I let my husband drive to town for supplies without me. After an hour in the sun, I stood and walked about. I chose my footing slowly and carefully on the rocks. I wasn't sure why, but it felt better to be moving. I walked to the base of the cliff and slowly began to pick my way up the steep slope. My feet sank into the soft sand, and my shoes filled with grit.

The view was startling. I could see a patchwork of brilliant colour in the ocean and lush rows of trees growing everywhere. All around me were bushes of hibiscus, and I picked some of the flowers, luxuriating in their bright colours. I saw more bushes further inland and made my way towards them, savouring the strong wind and the taste of the salt on my lips.

I stumbled across the remains of an old structure of some sort. The rocks had broken away from the mortar and lay separated in a loose line of rubble. The undergrowth had partially covered what was once a stone wall. I was standing there, trifling with a strand of grass, gazing at the reclaimed wilderness, when I noticed her. She stood near a mango tree. I caught a glimpse of her movement and felt that she had been watching me. Despite her dark colouring, I noticed her vivid blue eyes. She disappeared quickly and silently, before I could speak.

When my husband returned, we spent the evening together making dinner and reading. The rented timeshare had quickly begun to take on the clutter of our books and papers as we settled into routines transplanted from home. Scotch for him, white wine spritzer for me, and a long, quiet night together. Occasionally we might interrupt the other with something amusing from our reading, but more often we did not, preferring to keep our reading and thoughts to ourselves.

I opened a new book and was about to read the last few pages before I began the first chapter, when I saw her again. She was standing outside the un-curtained window, near the desk where my husband was seated. We made brief eye contact, and then she stepped backwards and melted into the darkness.

"So," I thought, "she knows where I am staying."

In bed, the moonlight kept me from sleeping. I wondered who she was and why she was walking about late at night. Eventually, when I did sleep, I dreamt of her. It was a vivid dream. She was married to a tall, handsome man. They lived in a two-room house on the large cliff by the sea, and there were savage storms, long rains, and, occasionally, treasured letters sent from far away. They had a child. A sturdy little boy with dark hair and large blue eyes. Her loneliness was abated only by the feel of his pudgy fingers and the weight of his small body clinging to her own.

My husband had risen before me and gone off somewhere to paint. I took my hat and a book and left for the beach. Established on a large sunny rock, I began to read. A large whiskered bull swam near the rocks, and I began to watch him. There was an air of self-importance about his expression that amused me. Gently, I eased closer until I could see him more clearly. Near at hand, the ocean seemed deeper and darker than I had expected, and the sound of the waves was so loud that it throbbed. I stared at the violence surging below and began to feel drawn to it. I lay down on the rocks and tried to touch the surf. The spray soaked me, and my fingers grew cold. I felt dazed. The bull was so close that I could see the markings on his snout. I wanted to join him in the water. I pulled back to give myself the leverage needed for dropping into the ocean. As I did so, I gashed my elbow on rock. The sudden sting of salt in the fresh wound halted me.

It was then that I realized my vulnerability. I had never learned to swim, and it would have been impossible for me to survive in that depth of water. The undertow and rocks would have worked rapidly. I pulled back from the edge and crawled across the rocks to the safety of the beach. I glimpsed her again at that moment. She was standing at the top of the cliff, her hands clasped in front of her, her brilliantly coloured clothes blown tightly against the outline of her body. Spray dripping from my hair ran into my eyes and caused me to blink. When I looked again, she was gone.

Trembling, I made my way back to the house. I sat on a chair and began to cry. I cried with a deep sense of emptiness and with longing for the dark-haired little boy in my dream. I was sitting there when my husband came in. He ran me a warm bath and brought me dry clothes. He sat on the toilet seat beside the tub while I soaked. I told him about wanting to climb off the rocks and into the ocean.

He was quiet at first. And when finally he spoke, he talked about our grieving. The words came out slowly and painfully, but his voice was gentle and I felt quieted by his closeness and by the naming of our sorrow. We went to the small bedroom, and held each other until sleep finally erased the sadness.

For the next week, we made a conscious effort to be together. We went for long walks along the beach, we drove to the remains of an old sugar plantation, and we visited the local waterfalls and souvenir shops. We took pictures of the wild roosters and chickens that seemed to roam freely all around the area.

Realizing that our time for finishing holiday projects was drawing to a close, I suggested that my husband take some painting time while I grocery shopped. The ride to town was uneventful, but I drove cautiously, focusing my attention on landmarks. In town, I shopped quickly. Driving home proved a challenge. The first few turns were evident and well marked, but then I began to question myself. In the bright light, the open roads and vegetation looked the same in every direction. There were an overwhelming number of turns that looked identical both left and right. As I crossed dusty intersections, I saw glimpses of the ocean in the distance. At other times, all I could see were masses of vibrant green swathed with streaks of yellow and red.

Far ahead, on the right, I saw a woman walking. Relieved, I drove towards her, hoping to confirm with her a sense of direction. As I gained on her, I noticed that she was barefoot and was wearing a beautiful sarong. Somehow I missed the moment when she veered off into the trees and I abruptly lost sight of her. And then I remembered the woman who had watched me at the beach and looked in at me at night, the woman who had appeared in my dream. I drove on, wary and uneasy. Finally, I spotted some familiar things including the tightly planted rows of tropical flowers leading to the resort.

The next few days were calm and productive. I busied myself with a flurry of paper work. I made elaborate dinners. We cuddled on the couch when reading, and our renewed intimacy made me feel vibrant and strong.

On our last full day, I decided to take a photograph of the seal colony. I went down to the beach. The seals were swimming close to the shoreline and I carefully selected the settings for my camera. I waited patiently for a well-composed shot. While I watched, I felt the spray on my face, arms, and legs. The diving and splashing of the seals looked effortless and carefree. By some sort of illusion of shadow and water and light, I thought suddenly that I could see a little boy in the waves with them. I was desperate to wade out into the cool liquid playground to touch him and lead him to shallow water. I heard my name. My husband had come to the beach. I waved at him eagerly.

That night, I dreamed about the little boy again. At first he was at the beach, splashing in the shallows. Then he walked out further and the water nuzzled the edge of his short pants until it completely covered his chubby knees. The tide turned swiftly while I watched, and he was quickly knocked over by the violent waves. I ran from the house, stumbled down the cliff, and pushed into the sea. The seals confused me. I would turn towards a sleek black head and it would plunge to the side. I couldn't see my little boy for all of the other black heads. I was fighting the waves when my husband woke me. We locked up and left at dawn.

Back at home, we returned to our regimen. My husband was completing a series of watercolours for a new show. His need to be alone was still there, but it was shorter-lived and didn't leave me feeling excluded as it once had. He reached for me at night when he slipped into bed, and I slid comfortably into the solid curl of his body.

A visit to the doctor confirmed that I was once again pregnant. From the first premonition of my new state, I could only ever think of the baby as *him*. My husband and I would lie together in bed trying to feel *his* little head or bottom pressing against me, watching to see a rippling movement in my swollen belly. Caressing and talking to *him* as he grew. But I was frightened also. Frightened to think that I had known this child before he had ever been conceived.

BLUE EYES

When he was born, after hours of struggling to emerge, he had dark, wet hair. His eyes, when they opened, were bright blue. And I saw him as he would look swimming in the ocean: patting the waves, eluding my grasp, and slipping away.

The Yellow House

AT THE EDGE OF THE LAKE, far from other farms and away from the village, is a creamy yellow brick house. It stands alone and proud with its faded paint and rotting gingerbread. Lake winds and harsh winters have softened its corners, and the house looks smoothed by time. The surrounding yard is overgrown with buckthorn and lilac bushes. I once took care to plant and nurture them, but with unwanted liberty they have become wild and misshapen. At some distance from the buildings is a small family plot with a rusted iron fence and worn grave-markers pressed into the ground.

My son is buried there. *Henry Parrish. Age 2yrs. 2mos. Son of Wm.& Elizabeth. 1864-66.* And my husband's stone is next to it. *Wm. Parrish. 1842-1875. Beloved.* I had them put the stone up after a few years. It was right to mark his life in that place.

We were married in November, once the crops were in. There wasn't much to it. He asked me after the Rogation supper. He said, "Libbie, I need a wife. I've bought two hundred acres from the Crown Agent, and my father has given me stock to get me started. I'll never say 'no' to you and you'll be free to run the house as you like. I'm building a wooden one first, and, one day, I'll build one out of brick. We'll have a good life together, Libbie. Will you say 'yes'?" Looking down at his polished-for-Sunday boots.

There was something attractive about his straightforwardness. Something exciting about being asked, about being told I could run the household as I liked. I was seventeen and chafed when my mother told me we were putting down pears or salting pork. To run things as I wanted seemed to me to be a kind of insurance on happiness. He was a nice enough young man from a hard-working family. Tall with light-brown hair and good features. His hands were over-sized like those of all the Parrish men, with wide, toughened palms. His shoulders were broad and well-developed, but his manner was so gentle that you were never afraid of his size. He and my brother James were friends. It was an easy decision. He came home with me and asked my father. Before nightfall, it was settled and I was engaged.

The excitement of wedding preparations and the anticipation of my new status more than made up for the fact that we had never courted as well as the times when I wondered if I was missing out on something. I looked forward to Sundays when, after service, William would come home with us and talk about the crops, the house, and the animals that were ours. After dinner, Father would suggest a drive, and we would climb into rigs and bump out to the land that William had cleared and seeded. He, my father, and James would stride about, gesticulating and admiring the progress of the wheat and oats, checking for midges or black stem rust.

We were married early one Saturday. I wore a white waist cut from a bolt of cloth my mother started embroidering when I was born. The same worked fabric was used for my underthings and nightwear. I also wore a dark grey wool skirt and jacket ordered from Miss Steel in Whitby. She came by coach to cut and fit it, and then posted me the outfit two weeks later. It was trimmed in brown velvet ribbon.

After the meal, William thanked my parents stiffly, as if saying, "Thank you for your hospitality," to strangers, and then he and my brother loaded his wagon with my trunk.

Father lifted me up into place and said, "Good luck, Son," to William, and they all waved at us while we drove away.

William, beside me, spoke, "Well, we did it, Libbie. We're off to a good start, I think. We'll manage."

"Yes, William, thank you. You've worked tremendously hard, Father says." And we turned up the rough lane that led to the little board house. Finally, I could go in and see William's handiwork. Inside all was orderly and quiet and tidy. William, and his mother, had thought of everything. A table and two ladder-back chairs, a small hearth, our new stove ordered from the catalogue, and the dish dresser that James had made for us. There was a new rocker by the fireplace with a woven hickory bark seat. A small bedroom had been sectioned off from the open living space, and a delicate heart had been carved on the pine headboard.

I began to unpack. Carrying small armfuls of things from the wagon to the house. Arranging things. Making the bed. Setting out crockery. Moving the preserves to the newly finished cold cellar. William appeared, carrying his jacket, with his sleeves rolled up, after a couple of hours. He looked nervous. "Is it all right, Libbie? Do you have what you need?" he asked.

"Yes, William. It's very fine. Thank you."

"I'm glad you like it, Libbie. It's not as fine as the brick house will be, but it's a good start. You only have to say if there's something you want." He continued, "Do you think we might find something to eat? I didn't eat much at your mother's."

William found a loaf of bread and some apple butter, while I unpacked the plates that Grandmother Heaslip had sent as a wedding gift. We had our tea at the kitchen table on our special dishes with no tablecloth. We ate quietly, uncomfortable with each other. Afterwards, William said that he had to check on the sheep. He went outside again, leaving me to clear up and get ready for bed. I combed out my hair, washed, changed, and climbed into bed to wait for him. I almost fell asleep waiting, he was gone so long. Finally I heard him return. He called out to me before entering our bedroom. "Is it all right now, Libbie? Can I come in?"

He undressed in a corner of the room with his back to me and got under the covers quickly, wearing long-johns. I had washed enough of these at home not to be surprised by the look of them, but I was nervous and began to laugh a little.

"What is it?"

"I don't know, exactly."

"Well, you've had a long day. Maybe you should go to sleep now."

"But William..."

"Yes?"

"Aren't you going to do anything?"

"No, Libbie. Not tonight. Let's get some sleep."

When I woke in the morning, he was already gone. I saw that he had made his own breakfast and had left the dirty things in the dishpan. A clean plate on the table contained slices of fried potato, bread, and egg. I ate the cold breakfast and wondered what time it was. I dressed quickly, and went outside to find him. It was Sunday and I didn't want to be late for church.

William was in the barn. "Good morning, Lib," he grinned, "Did you sleep well?"

"Oh, William. I'm sorry. What time of day is it? What about church?"

"Almost noon. No one really expects us at church today. Let's do something special. What would you like?"

I was disappointed to have missed church. I had looked forward to walking in on William's arm and sitting beside him. Sharing the prayer book. Knowing that everyone thought that I had chosen wisely. I answered, "Anything, William. Whatever you would like."

"Well, I'd like to walk you around the farm. All of it. Would that be all right, Libbie?"

And so we walked around our fence-line. And William talked about the crops and the sheep and our small savings account, and the brick house he planned to build, and his brother's new plow. As I listened to him, I could see that he was happy. But finally, when I did speak, I said the wrong thing: "Is this all there is?"

"The farm, Libbie?"

"No, Will. Being married. Is this all there is to being married?"

Will stopped walking and looked around the field and down at the ground. "Well, Libbie, to tell you the truth, I don't know. I thought it meant just getting on. I don't know much more than that." He looked away and out at his fields again.

"I know, Will. I didn't mean to hurt you. I just don't feel any different."

"I'm sorry, Libbie. I'll try to get it right."

And when I had the courage to look at him, I saw that his eyes and eyelashes were wet. And I saw that he wasn't ashamed to let me see. And then I cried too. Both of us walked back to the house, sniffling like two scared children. Will helped in the kitchen. He showed me how to use the stove, and he cleaned the vegetables for dinner. When it was time for bed, Will said he was going to the barn. I asked him not to, and he said, "Libbie, I just don't know how to do this. I don't know what husbands do."

I grabbed at his shirt and said, "Just stay close, Will. Stay here with me." And he stayed. And we discovered a way to feel comforted together. Afterwards, Will went to the kitchen and heated water, and carried a large pan of it back to our room. Ever so gently, he sponged clean the sticky places on my legs. And he kissed me where I hurt a little and rubbed the sore place with his fingers.

From then on, every Sunday, no matter what the weather, we put on our outdoor things and walked the farm together after church. We established small routines. And I learned to feel satisfaction when I was able to produce my own pies or put out a meal for the men. By Epiphany, we knew I was with child.

When the time came for my ordeal, Will stayed with me. After a long night of struggling, Mrs. Cooper, the midwife, told us the baby was stuck. James went for Dr. Naysmith. The Doctor laid me on my side, and Will held onto my leg while the Doctor reached in with forceps to turn the baby. Pulling on the head, he guided him out. He arrived like a little swimmer, hands first, screaming angrily. Something ripped inside of me, and we knew right then that there wouldn't be any more. But the baby was wonderful and made the funniest little sounds. It was Will that held him first and tied the navel string, and named him Henry.

The first night, Henry slept between us in the big bed. Will kept unwrapping him to check his breathing. We were filled with wonder at his perfectly formed parts: at the chest that moved, at the fists that clenched our fingers, at the soft sounds he made. And, for a time, we were happy. Will bathed him and washed his hair and trimmed his tiny fingernails by chewing them off gently in his mouth. I loved the feel of his strong little body. I loved to watch him eat and sleep. I loved the sound of the words that came from his sweet mouth.

Diptheria came to the township when Henry was two. Will told me to stay at home, and not to let anybody visit. But I was young, and I believed that the diptheria was spread by kissing. One day when Will was off cutting hay, I hitched up the buggy, and I took Henry to Port. I never told Will. It started with a sore throat and coughing. I thought it was the croup. And then Henry said "hurts" when I tried to get him to take in some warm milk, and his little eyes filled with tears. Will got Dr. Naysmith to come. But it was already too late. A film of mucus had formed in his throat. The doctor lanced it with a feather and some silver nitrate, but we couldn't get any nourishment into him. He died within the week. Will held him that whole time.

Doctor Naysmith told us that the cows sometimes get the disease and pass it on in their milk. Will never said a word.

He put Henry down on the bed and went outside. The next thing I heard was James telling someone that Will had shot our dairy cow. A distancing set in while we were grieving, and it never went away.

In the evenings, Will had a pipe. I'd see him head towards our small cemetery with it. I went out to join him a couple of times, but I felt like I wasn't welcome. He needed to be alone in his grief. And so our visits there were separate. Will drove himself hard. He hired himself out for odd jobs in the winter. He helped put the road through to Lindsay one summer, and, all the while, he managed our own place. One spring, after the wheat was in, Will and James went to work with the stone-hookers in Port Whitby. They poled out on scows and scooped up, with long-handled rakes, shale from the lake bottom. The gathered stone was taken to Toronto, where it was used for sidewalks and construction. It paid well. They worked until early winter, when we got the first skiff of snow. Will hired his youngest brother, Richard, to run the farm and look in on me. The money Will made paid for the brick house. It was built the following year.

The house was all that Will had promised. Two-storey, yellow brick, with a front porch and a small bay window. We ordered patterned flooring and wallpaper for the front room. I spent weeks sewing rows and rows of fussy ruffles for the curtains. It was very grand. Upstairs, we had several large, empty rooms. Will's brother, Richard, moved in to the tiny wooden house to help manage our growing herds.

It never occurred to me, back then, to consider Will's feelings for me, or my feelings for him either. We got on, and that was all. But Richard caused trouble to start. He was always buzzing around trying to help me in the kitchen with women's work. And then one night, Will came to dinner alone and said we were to start without Richard. I asked after him and Will said that he was in Toronto looking at some farm implements. I was hurt not to have been told. I said to Will that I didn't think it was friendly of Richard to leave without saying "goodbye."

"Libbie, you've spoiled that boy for others, you know," he replied. "Do you not intend for him to marry one day and find his own bit of happiness?"

"As if marrying could make someone happy," I snapped.

"I'm sorry you're not happy, Elizabeth. I've tried to do right by you. I know it's my fault the boy died, and I've given up hope that you'll get over it."

"Your fault, Will? Why was it your fault?" I felt a cold chill brush over me. Something dreadful was happening between us and I couldn't make it stop.

"The cow was my fault. I should have had her checked."

"Will, it's no more your fault than mine. I was the one who took him to Port Perry."

"What?" A long pause. "You did what?"

"Will, it was a long time ago. Let's not talk about it and make matters worse."

"Tell me, Elizabeth," he raised his voice, "you did what?"

"Port Perry. I took him to Port Perry."

Will was quiet. His hands were gripping the table's edge. He stood up slowly, looking down at his plate. Trembling.

"All of these years," he began, "all of these years, I have tried to make amends. I blamed myself for what happened and thought that you would never forgive me. And now, now you tell me this. I had a right to know, Libbie. I had a right..." He broke off and walked to the outside door. It was snowing and I called after him, but he went outside without answering.

I moved the lamps and set them by the windows. And I sat up through the night, waiting for him. By morning, he had not come back inside, and so I wrapped up and went to the barn. The horse and cutter were in their places, but there was no sign of Will. I found some partially covered footsteps heading to the cemetery. The snow had blown hard in the night, but Henry's grave had clear evidence of Will's visit. The steps continued from there to the lake edge and seemed to go straight out onto the ice.

I ran back to the barn, and drove the sleigh to James' place. James came back with me. He took a hoe and a rope and walked out onto the ice. He walked carefully and slowly, tapping the hoe ahead of his steps. He turned around after a bit and carefully picked his way back to shore. He shook his head when he reached me. "The ice is broken, Lib. There are footsteps leading to the break. I'm sorry." He took me in his arms and guided me back to the house. "He must have got lost in the snow. I can't think what else might have happened."

I dream sometimes that Will survived the icy water and swam to shore. If this is true, I'm sure he'll go back, as I must also do, to take my place inside the iron fence. I will stand there, at first, and touch the letters, and my hands will caress the cold stone. I will study the house, which is no longer mine, and wonder what small tokens of my life were left to mark the walls or litter the empty rooms. And then I will lie down beside my son, in view of the house, the lake, and the garden, and I will wait for Will.

Blue Mountain

THERE'S A SPRING ON THE SIDE of the mountain that gushes cold from a crevice in the rock. We drank there together—me lapping from your cupped hands, my tongue tasting the salt of your skin. The searing heat wilted me, and I lay down in deep shade, my head supported by your legs. How like the mountain you were to me, steady and solid, with your own weather and turnings, full of surprise and mystery.

There was a castle there once, built with rock from the mountain and hidden from view. Farmers looted the stone for their barns and sheds until the remains finally crumbled, and the castle fell. The farmers returned to cull the last of the stone and carry away pieces of the fairytale. And the castle stones remain on the mountain, pushed firmly into place and obscured in walls of fieldstone and rubble. We laughed at the utility of those unromantic souls grasping at pieces of magic for their barns.

A blue haze mists the peaks in the morning. As a child, I was intrigued by the blurring of edges. "Where did it go?" I would wonder as we approached what should have been a cloudy fog of light and magic, but was instead a clear and sunny vista with soft winds blowing at our hair and faces.

But the mountain was not where I fell in love. Rather, it was in the art gallery. You speaking about Robert Motherwell's Spanish Elegies, dressed in gold cords and a tweed blazer—summoning the eloquence of his brush strokes and convincing the small assembled group following us that our lives would never be the same if we meditated on the large black shapes and responded with our hearts. And as I watched you striding through the gallery—confident and intent on the work, gesturing to the genius—I suddenly saw the movement and tension in the painted forms.

All of my pieces, we used to say. *You know all of my pieces.*

The *fading away* was gradual, a leaking of energy and sound. The tremors were almost indiscernible. A shaking hand in the morning while you filled our cups with coffee. Your even handwriting suddenly spiking and wavering, a confident signature becoming illegible. Somehow your hand would no longer grip with certainty a pen or fine marker. We would look at each other and then quickly turn away, not willing to name our fear.

One day you were driving and forgot the way home. We made a joke of it. Laughed about the new building going up, and the increase in traffic. *It could happen to anyone.* That night, we held hands in the gloaming, not speaking.

The doctor prescribed medication to minimize the trembling. We read aloud to each other in the evening to strengthen your vocal chords, to prolong the muscle tone that allowed you to swallow and speak. But the meds made you sleepy, childlike in your need for naps and quiet rests. And I was suddenly alone in our shared home.

Fumbling fingers came next. Shirt buttons eluded you. Zippers became a challenge, the small metal tab too tiny for your awkward touch. We tried leaving pins to hook the zipper up or down beside the sink, but hooking the tab with a pin proved equally challenging. You would stand there, defeated, in our small bathroom, warm liquid running down your legs while you struggled. And another indignity had to be born. You stopped reading your beloved books on art, unable to turn the pages, the heft of them too much to hold. We did not discuss these things, fearful that the speaking of them would lock them in. Instead, we quietly adjusted, resigned to the silent encroachment of the disease.

In moments of clarity, you would speak softly and slowly, and I would strain to make out your words. You encouraged me to write down the combination to the safe, the location of our insurance policies, the name of our accountant. You guided the small practical preparations that could be made, and we left unspoken the things that we could not know to prepare for. The microwave eluded you, as did the remote for the television. Your fingers became too rigid for the computer keyboard. Your movements stiffened, and our evening walks eased into a slow shuffle.

On the first day that I drove you to the Manor and left you there in a ghastly yellow room, I could not bear to stay. I went to the mountain and searched for our spring, but the landmarks had shifted and I could not find it. I pulled over and turned off the ignition. Determined, I began to walk along the steep gravel road, searching for cut rock in the foundations of barns.

While I walked, birdsong and cicadas sounded, and the sweet air came to me, smelling of fresh cut hay and spring earth redolent with promise. And I saw that square bales stood in quilted fields like temporal sentries, and the bright bay sparkled in the distance with toy boats dotting the turquoise surface. The castle rocks eluded me, and I returned to the car.

The Shoe Tree

THE FIRST SHOE TREE THEY SAW was in the airport lands. Century farms had been expropriated and now formed a large park, rich fields waiting to be covered by runways and hangars. They drove by overgrown lilac bushes and crippled orchards. And then, inconceivably, on the side of the road was an old maple, its girth wide, covered in sneakers and shoes. They stopped the car. The shoes were nailed in pairs, pointing skyward. Children's shoes, adult runners, footwear in all sizes and colours and styles, covering the bark from the ground to where the crown began to spread, a good twelve feet up.

It became their thing to spot these trees. They searched the internet for locations and drove through the country on weekends to photograph them. They weren't particularly beautiful, just quirky and a little ludicrous. Some of the websites referred to them as an *art form*. Others referenced them as *a place where old shoes go to die*. The American version had them hanging by shoelaces from tree branches, swung into place. The trees remained fascinating in all of their incarnations. They were usually found on quiet dirt roads, away from the bustle of traffic. Sometimes, they brought a picnic or went into a local convenience store for bottled water and a bag of potato chips. There was a small sense of victory each time they located one, as though they had claimed it for their own.

They never touched the shoes. They never stood close enough to examine them or to speculate about the owners. They never wondered about the lives of those who had worn the shoes. They never allowed themselves to get a sense of anything other than the novelty of the shoe tree itself. Sometimes they would count the shoes half-heartedly, in a vague attempt to calculate the total number of shoes on a tree and the approximate value of the discarded footwear. They talked about starting a website for shoe-tree spotters. They planned a society for them. They discussed publishing their book of photographs. They would establish themselves and make their mark on the world as the first shoe-tree experts

They drove to small towns and villages and to cottage country and they planned their holidays around forays to the States where American versions dotted the highways. They shared their obsession with no one. They printed their photographs as eight by ten glossies and slipped them into page protectors, saved in a binder and labelled with the location and date of each photograph. Late at night, they would open the binder and flip through the plastic pages, glancing at their collection. The trees, in many ways, told the story of their burgeoning relationship: their travels, their picnics, their road trips. All neatly preserved in the documentary binder.

In restaurants, she would slip her foot inside his trouser leg. Later, she would remove his socks and trousers and continue along the path of her foot, licking him until they both grew wet. Their lovemaking was fuelled by their joint obsession. He would fondle her feet, suckle her toes, and massage her calves. Slowly, he would move his hands up and along the trunk of her body, pulling her towards him until they merged in a private frenzy.

En route to a party one night, they cut through the airport lands to pass by their first shoe tree. They slowed down as they drew near. The tree had been stripped and was now swathed in yellow plastic ribbon. A small sign had been posted by the airport authority, stating that they had removed the shoes in an effort to preserve the tree. The irony of this was a personal affront. They raged.

That night, alone and once more in her small apartment, they ended. "It's over now," he said.

At first she thought he meant only the shoe trees. But the look of him made it clear. He had kicked off his loafers earlier in the evening, and she bent down slowly to pick them up. He left in his sock feet.

The Whale Watcher

YOU CAN CALL ME THE WHALE WATCHER. I'd like that. I'm thirty-two years old, and pretty much keep to myself. I live in a condo near the Hill and I chain-smoke, even though this is no longer socially acceptable. My friend, Arnie, who runs a pet store, is always telling me I should quit, "for the sake of the fish." I have two pair of Nishikigoi. Most people call them koi. One pair, in the hall tank, is Bekko. They're the white ones with black markings. The other pair is Asagi. They're mostly grey and blue above the lateral line but are bright red and orange underneath. The Asagi and their delicately coloured scales are my favourite. I call them Ahab and Jonah. They keep me company. But of late, they have taken to peering at me with their huge eyes, and so I've had to start undressing in the bathroom.

Three years ago I took my holidays in the fall. I wanted to do something different on my vacation and needed to find something I could do alone. The travel agency had a brochure on New England. I flew down, rented a car, and stayed at a bed-and-breakfast on the shore. It was painted bright blue and sat on the edge of a cliff, fronting a small salt bay.

At breakfast (eggs sunny-side up, French toast, and coffee), the proprietor came over to my table and sat down in the facing wicker chair. Enormous eyebrows sprung from just below his forehead, with the odd thick white hair jabbing out crazily. "You meetin' someone down here?" he asked.

Surprised, I answered without thinking. "No, my boyfriend was busy. And I needed a rest." I hoped that I looked sufficiently fatigued.

"So, what does he do?"

"Um, accountant. He's an accountant."

"That's a good job, eh. You gonna' get married?"

"Well, yes, someday. I suppose so."

"Me and Irene, we been married twenty-seven years. Three boys and five grandchildren, we got."

He looked at me, expecting a response. Congratulations perhaps? I changed the subject. "What do you recommend tourists do for entertainment?"

"Well, lemme see," he offered, "there's the whales. Every day a boat goes out with whale watchers. Researchers from the marine place. They takes them."

The next morning, equipped with a hand drawn map, and a borrowed slicker, I set off for the docks. I found the boat and paid forty dollars to someone in a plywood kiosk near the wharf. I moved toward the small collection of tourists crowded near a metal ramp and waited to embark. The boat looked rather like a small, worn ferry. It was gaily painted in thick layers of lumpy red and white and yellow. Although it was not particularly large, we all found a seat. Someone rang an old-fashioned bell, and with a huge jerk and rocking motion, we began to move. Downstairs a slide show was scheduled to begin. Holding on to the railing tightly, I picked my way down the metal stairs. There was a recorded lecture as well.

Welcome to the Armagh and thank you for joining us here. Your support subsidizes our research at the Margate School of Oceanography and allows us to continue studying the migratory patterns of the Humpback whales. Humpbacks, as they are commonly known, are baleen whales belonging to the Balaenopteridae family. They can measure up to fifty feet in length and may weigh as much as forty tons. They migrate from the northern latitudes where they summer, to the southern climates where they winter. Humpbacks are easy whales to identify because they flip their tales in a kind of farewell wave before they dive. And, while they are slow swimmers, they are extremely active, and can often be seen breaching, flippering, or lobtrailing. Individual whales can be readily identified by the unique pattern of markings on their tail flukes. One of the interesting characteristics of the Humpback is the long complicated song that the males take turns singing. It is believed that this song is in some way related to an act of courtship....

While the lecture droned on, I studied my fellow passengers and rubbed my fingers on the circulating baleen. We travelled on the open water for two hours. Several people threw up in the tiny bathroom. To escape the smell, I went on deck where it was cold and damp and monotonous.

Suddenly, there was a shout. "There they are!"

"Cut!" yelled someone else. The engine stopped and suddenly there was silence as we drifted. No one spoke. We looked at each other expectantly. Some readied their cameras hopefully.

"Over here," called a voice.

We rushed to the sound of the voice and as we did so, the boat lurched sharply. Staff cautioned us to spread ourselves out evenly. I stood by myself—far from the others—clinging to the railing. "Stay put!" yelled one of the oceanographers. "He's only being friendly," added another.

"He's scraping off barnacles," explained the captain. "We're perfectly safe. Don't panic."

"My God," screamed a woman, "he's trying to kill us! He'll crush the boat! We'll die!"

Panicky and nauseous, I continued to cling to the railing. I could not have moved if I wanted to. While I stood there, a dark shadow appeared under the surface. The colour got darker quickly, and it rose to the surface. It was a textured rubber back with molluscs and sea plants attached. Water slid from it as it nuzzled against the hull. If I had dared to let go of the railing, I could have touched it with my fingers. For several seconds, it remained there, watching me. Then quietly and quickly it submerged, leaving nothing but the sound of the ocean rushing to cover it.

"That was Santayana," offered a researcher. "We call him the Philosopher. He's gentle."

My whale had a name. A philosopher whale. A gentle whale. With the others, I crowded around the rails and searched eagerly for another glimpse of him. From a distance, we watched the whales at their leisure. They avoided the Armagh, and we bobbed gently while the researchers took notes and photographs. I was disappointed when the engine started and the ride back to shore began.

When I returned to the bed and breakfast, Irene greeted me with a bowl of steaming chowder. "I thought you'd be wet through," she said, "and in need of a warm cuppa'. Did ya' enjoy yourself, now?"

I took the chowder gratefully and answered in the affirmative. "Well, eat up, girl and come downstairs. Reuel is building a fire and it'll be snug in the living room." I ate the chowder, changed into some warm dry clothes, and went downstairs. There was a collection of delicately figured blue-and-white china in the open shelves of a small hutch.

"Ballast from the boats," said Reuel. "In th' old days, they used it in clippers coming from th' Orient. We found it in our cellar when we were replacing a footing. Th' rest we collected round about. S'mostly all gone now."

We ate a late dinner in the living room and retired shortly afterwards. I was the only guest. The next day, with encouragement from my hosts, I visited the Clipper Museum. The following day, I drove to another town and toured houses that had once belonged to sea captains. I also drove to Nantucket and visited the tourist sites there. The week sped by in a study of the whaling industry and clipper ships. Irene and Reuel were congenial hosts and prepared delicious meals.

When it was time to leave, I packed my things, including many trashy souvenirs, bid Irene and Reuel good-bye, and headed back to my life of spreadsheets and tax forms. It had been a satisfying vacation and had given me much to ponder. On a whim, I booked tickets to Boston for the Canadian Thanksgiving weekend. I stayed with Irene and Reuel again, and enjoyed the familiarity with which they greeted me. I liked the pink-and-green guest room that I was beginning to think of as "mine." The room was soft and quiet without being fussy. It was a welcome contrast to my sand-beige condo and sterile grey cubicle.

Reuel brought up the whales at dinner. "You've caught the itch for things remote," he said. "The whales do that. But what about that accountant? Where is he now?"

"Still busy," I answered. "But we're moving to another level."

"Ah," said Reuel pondering. "Is that what they call it now?"

My weekend passed quickly, and I was sorry to leave for the airport. On almost every long weekend and holiday after that, I sought out whale-related excursions. I went to Baja, and to the British Columbia coast, and was saving for Hawaii. I spent money liberally on every sightseeing tour and whale souvenir I could find. My special talisman was a tiny wooden whale that opened its mouth to reveal an even tinier Pinocchio. I kept this on my desk. Who knows what's on the inside, I thought. Numbers don't tell the whole story.

Colleagues began to think me more eccentric than usual. My quiet ways had always provoked gentle teasing, but somehow the whale watching marked me as a complete outsider. A married lover with small children would have been more readily understood and more easily forgiven. I returned to Reuel and Irene's the following two summers. I learned the names of the crew on the Armagh, and came to recognize tail fluke markings without the assistance of the photos.

And then, on a particularly grey and foggy day, I saw my whale again. Santayana. He swam close to the boat, surfaced and submerged, and then resurfaced at the other end of the boat. My hair was wet from the fog and spray, salt had stung my lips and face and eyes, and I was chilled right through with ocean. And that moment was enough for me. The next morning, I told Reuel and Irene that I had to get back early. While parting, I hugged them both farewell.

Later, while walking through the airport's maze of tunnels and shopping concourses, I stopped to shift my luggage. The pot lights in a small window attracted me. Moving closer, I saw that some beautiful jewellery had been laid out on velvet. An officious gentleman bid me enter the shop, and I did. "Madame," he said, "how may I be of assistance?"

"Just looking, thanks," I murmured.

"A ring perhaps?" he offered. "Worn on the right hand, they are also exquisite."

I felt exposed. My empty ring finger had left me vulnerable. "No thank you," I replied, "I couldn't possibly do this alone."

"Surely," he said, "anyone would enjoy a *slight* economy. I can offer you a thirty percent discount on any ring. Here, let me show you." He pulled a chain of keys from his pocket and unlocked the display. "Your hand," he commanded. I extended my left hand. He slipped on a large solitaire. I could not bear to take it off. I left the store marked as an engaged woman. Someone had claimed me.

Gridlock

SHE IS WEARING A DOLLAR STORE TIARA, and we can just see the top of a pink sequined dress—likely a ballet dress or a princess costume. Her black bangs are combed across her forehead, and her dark eyes shine brightly as she bounces a little in her seat. We are caught in what appears to be gridlock, and the secondary fan has just kicked in. Trying to keep our car from overheating, we have turned off the air conditioning and opened the windows.

The open windows have somehow made us more vulnerable, more aware of the congestion of the city. Cyclists are stopped alongside the cars, discretely balancing themselves with one hand on the rear flanks of nearby vehicles. Pedestrians are congregated at the corners, waiting to cross at the intersection, and straining to see what the difficulty is, where the accident is, what the hold-up is. I place my purse on the floor between my feet, concerned that someone could easily reach in and pluck it from my lap.

There are two policemen in the middle of the intersection, directing traffic. They arrived on bicycles, wearing shorts. The stoplights are working, but they are ignoring these and yelling directions at drivers and pedestrians alike. They seem stressed and angry. They speak into walkie-talkies. Collectively, we listen intently, trying to determine where they would like us to move and why.

The car in front of our queue attempts an illegal right turn and is screamed at by the young officer. Slowly the driver reverses his car, and awkwardly re-positions himself at the front of our line. We have not yet crept forward to claim the additional six feet of pavement. We wait, impatient and frustrated, trying to understand why we are locked here.

And then it slowly becomes clear. Two police motorcycles approach, followed by a police car with flashing lights. "A politician," states my partner with contempt. "We've all been sitting here in the heat waiting for the f-ing premier to drive by."

My eyes cast over the sidewalk crowd, and I see that some of them have also sensed this. They are waving at the motorcade of black cars that is now moving towards us. A parade of large black limos. But then I see the two policemen saluting. Rigid. Standing at attention. A hearse appears and the crowd quietens.

"Of course," I think suddenly, "a fallen soldier."

"What an insult," sputters my mate. "Why do they call the trip to the morgue the Highway of Heroes? It's an insult. Why not pick a beautiful road or a national highway? The trip to the morgue? It's ludicrous. What a lack of imagination."

"It's moving," I respond. "The families find it moving. And helpful."

"I'm not denigrating that aspect," he fumed, "it's just the whole Highway of Heroes thing. Why couldn't they pick something less ironic?"

"It's a way to mark gratitude," I respond gently. "It's the least we can do for their families."

"It's not a war we should be fighting. We don't belong there and those boys don't belong there. Canadians should not be dying there."

"But we are there," I say, "and the nation needs to mourn."

"Not like this," he answered, shifting the car into drive, and accelerating slightly. "Not like this."

I look over at the adjacent car and get a final glimpse of the little girl. She surveys the roadway happily as her car also moves forward. She is still bouncing a little. Untouched by the young man who has died before his time and the pain of those left behind. I press the button to close my window while my partner turns on the air.

Roadside

CINDY SAW A LONE DISCARDED TEDDY BEAR at the corner of Balsam and Fir. Perhaps tossed from a window by a small child, she speculated, while pausing at the intersection for the light to change.

Driving home again at the end of the afternoon, she glanced over and saw that someone had propped up the teddy. Leaned it against a hydro pole, helpfully. Someone will be able to see it now, she thought. There's bound to be a frantic parent trying to satisfy an unhappy child somewhere. Tears in the back seat.

In the morning, the bear was garrotted to the pole, roped by a cord around its neck, suspended five feet in the air. A small pyre of drugstore carnations, still wrapped in cellophane, was piled on the ground underneath. An offering to teddy, was Cindy's first thought.

Cindy was a career coach and met her clients in Tim Hortons and McDonalds all over the city. One-hour counselling sessions over breakfast sandwiches or the soup of the day. Her office was a wireless laptop and a Blackberry. Her first client met her at seven am in a quiet Scarborough Tim's. He was a shy banker in his forties who had been passed over for promotion. A quick look at him—dejected, over-weight, cheap ill-fitting suit—told Cindy the entire story while she stood at the counter waiting for her bag-in, steeped tea. The first thing they would need to do is buy the best-tailored suit he could afford. Followed by a gym membership. Confidence building and key messaging would follow.

"Three months," Cindy said, sitting down across from him. "You can have the job you want in three months."

"How do you know that?" he asked her sceptically, but with something else—a flash of excitement perhaps—edging his words.

"It's my job to know," Cindy said. "Once I teach you your value, and you convey that value using simple key messages, they'll be asking themselves why they didn't promote you sooner."

Cindy's second appointment was at a local broadcast studio. She was working with a newly hired newscaster to help "even out her confidence levels." Her voice shook when she became agitated. She had two weeks to help her breathe and regulate her anxiety.

From there, Cindy drove to her third session of the day, in a small McDonalds she had deliberately chosen, with a very polished and arrogant young man named Jeffery. His mentor had called Cindy and asked her to make him a priority. Jeffery was a bright and competent super-star, but he was so ambitious and insincere that nobody was able to work with him. His colleagues distrusted him. His clients found him superficial.

"We need to work on your small talk," Cindy began. "Facility with conversation will put people at ease and help you to convey the warmer side of your personality."

Jeffery nodded. Spread beside him were an expensive briefcase, the opened stock market pages of the *Globe and Mail*, and his cell phone. He glanced at his watch and adjusted his long legs in the cramped space. Although he had purchased a coffee, he had pushed it away from him in evident distaste. His body language conveyed disdain—both his arms and his legs were crossed, and he was leaning away from Cindy in the small booth. His face wore a forced smile that was rather like an unpleasant grimace.

"We will work on your body language next week," said Cindy. "I will send you a copy of some articles to read before our next session. I will also send you a short activity to practice."

"All right," said Jeffery, "now what?"

"Now we begin a conversation," said Cindy. "Give me a topic that you would like to discuss. Something social."

"I can't think of anything," he responded. "You pick."

"All right," said Cindy, "I will. I saw a teddy bear abandoned at an intersection yesterday. At first I thought it was a child's toy, thrown from the window. But, this morning, I saw flowers piled underneath it. It looked like one of those roadside shrines that sometimes crop up after an accident."

"I dislike those," retorted Jeffery. "They are distracting and don't belong in public places."

"Where do you think they belong, Jeffery?" she asked, prompting him.

"In funeral homes. Keep everything together. Do it all at once and get it over with. That's the point of a funeral," he answered.

"I see," Cindy replied. "So you don't think there is a place for public displays of grief?"

"No, not at all. Why should the rest of us have that imposed on us? Why should our tax dollars pay to clean up the mess?"

"When Princess Diana died, Buckingham Palace was covered in flowers. Were all of those people wrong to litter?"

"That's not what I'm saying," Jeffery replied, petulant. "It was different; she was a princess."

"Why, Jeffery? Why is it different?" continued Cindy, stiffening in response to him. Feeling irritable suddenly and no longer wishing to continue.

"It just was," replied Jeffery. "Are we done yet?"

"Yes," said Cindy, smiling at him politely, "Yes, Jeffery, we are done. I'm sorry but I really can't help you. You will need to find another coach. I'll email you some names. Good luck."

Cindy stood at this, picked up her purse, and left without shaking his hand or waiting for him to stand. She walked back to her car quickly and sat inside trembling. It wasn't often that she encountered a client she could not work with. But if she kept only those clients she felt empathy for, she would soon lose valuable contracts. Ratios of success and failure. *How to reconcile those she empowered with those she cast off.*

Driving home, she slowed down at the intersection and saw that more flowers and stuffed animals had been left with the teddy. A much-loved child had died, and the evidence of grief confirmed her resolve. *Tomorrow she would also leave something behind.*

Mrs. Harris

IN THE MIDST OF OUR POST-WAR SALTBOXES with knee-high hedges and borders of brightly coloured annuals, there was a small grey tarpaper house. It was iced with white gingerbread, a lacy wooden porch and a matching picket fence. The Harris house was a remnant from an earlier farming settlement, and it had been preserved, incongruously, in the midst of what was to become, during my adolescence, a thriving section of the city, with its own subway stop.

The Harris house was unusual in other respects. Unlike our smartly groomed patches of lawn and tidy cemented pathways, it was surrounded by a proliferation of weeds and wildflowers. Mrs. Harris showed us no mercy when an errant volleyball or badminton birdie strayed into her territory. She claimed these as weapons in an undeclared war against her *preshus purrennials* and would not relinquish them, no matter how polite our entreaties. I had visions of her, late at night, wearing a long cotton nightie, batting her prizes about with silent satisfaction. Touching our lost toys with glee.

"Let 'er have 'em," we had agreed. "She needs 'em worse than we do." But occasionally, with the loss of a new Frisbee just a little too fresh, we'd complain to a parent.

"Serves you right," was the typical rejoinder. "You kids can play somewhere else."

Halloween was the night of all nights in our neighbourhood. It was the one night when, in an era before poisoned fruit and razor blades, we were allowed to run unfettered. We returned home just long enough to dump the contents of our decorated apple baskets into the waiting pyrex bowl, and ventured out again to collect more. It was our unfounded hope that Mrs. Harris would come to the door bearing birdies and basketballs and not simply the stale, loose cup of popcorn she was known to dump, unceremoniously, into our baskets.

Mrs. Harris was what our parents, in the privacy of dining rooms during weekly card parties, called a "Bible thumper." She carried a large black leather Bible under her arm on Sundays and Wednesdays, when she emerged from her front door and strode purposefully down the street to a little Pentecostal Chapel about a mile away. She often assailed one of us en route, asking if we had heard of Hell or a particular mission in Africa. My friends backed away from her during these exchanges, leaving me alone to mumble polite apologies.

I was one of the *foreigner's daughters*. There were three of us. My eldest sister was a pale and delicate anomaly, her manner quiet and deferential. My second sister was an olive-skinned daredevil who wore tight pedal pushers and had amazingly long eyelashes. And then there was me, the third child, plain and chubby with long black hair and eyes too big for her face. She thought we were *exotic*. I heard her say so to Mrs. Scott one day, as if I were invisible, playing hopscotch on the very next square of sidewalk.

We were *Catholic exotics* in a neighbourhood that housed mostly United Church, Presbyterians, and Mrs. Harris' particular blend of righteous Gospel. I can still summon her: marching with beige orthopaedic shoes tightly laced, a flowered dress partially covered by a white cardigan done up to the neck, a straw bowler perched on neatly permed blue-grey hair, a handkerchief wrapped around the handle of her vinyl handbag, and a large Bible clutched to her flat chest. The outfit varied only in winter, when she slipped into fur-trimmed ankle boots, a wine-coloured wool coat, and donned a diminutive mink cap.

Summers have slipped one into the other, and our lemonade stands, maple key dances, and willow whip wars blur together into a childhood filled with play and laughter. It was a safe community where anyone's parent would feed you dinner, bandage a scraped knee or call home if you were caught being *saucy*. Mrs. Harris' death was a turning point.

The adults noticed that she wasn't going to church anymore. They assumed she was sickly. Mr. Cooper tried to phone, but her phone was disconnected. When he called in on her, she said that she didn't need a phone, as there was no one left to call and she never used it. He reported that she seemed frail. Our mothers immediately made soup and casseroles and carried them over. She met them at the door and said that she didn't need charity. She refused their offerings and shut the door on them. She offended us all in this way.

Then it was noticed that her lights weren't going on in the evenings. Again, Mr. Cooper was dispatched to call on her. She primly informed him that her habits had changed and that she was now retiring early and had no need to squander hydro-electricity. The adults were amused by her thrift, and she was once again left without intrusion.

Weeks passed and then it was then noticed that no laundry appeared on her clothesline, and that her drapes remained tightly shut. Assuming that she had certainly fallen ill, Mr. Cooper walked up to her front door and knocked. When there was no reply, he motioned to Mr. Flynn, and together they forced open a window and climbed inside. The smell, they said, was terrible. Mr. Flynn, a tall auto-mechanic with Popeye arms and a loud laugh, staggered outside and threw up.

We watched with interest when the white van came from her church. They packed up everything and emptied the house. She had left her belongings to a Leprosy Mission. They put plywood sheets on the windows and doors and mowed down her garden. "Would she ever be mad to see that!" we commented.

"I guess the church is getting all our stuff," said one of my friends. "Think we could ask for it?"

But we knew better than to ask. Instead, we stared while the church people tidied up and drove off. We did not trespass once she was gone. When a birdie was lobbed too hard, we let it rest in her devastated garden. When the cherries ripened on her tree, we looked at them but did not take the fruit. There was a silent accord among us. Shame settled like a heavy fog. Our parents continued to ask the lingering question: *how did this happen?*

When I think about that time, I realize that her passing provided a first glimmer of what we would later recognize as our own parents' fallibility. They had not protected us from what was, in the end, her witness.

Romaine Hearts

OUR NEIGHBOURHOOD WAS IN a protected enclave—two facing rows of houses bordered by fields, a church, and a row of shops. A creek bed kept the fields sodden and marshy, and for our play, we were limited to a stretch of homes and backyards bordered by old maples and over-sized willows. We took pride in knowing things. Our secrets gave us a sense of leverage over the adults who so tightly ruled us.

"Keith knows something!" was a summoning that made us readily abandon our pursuits and huddle in close.

"Bird's Nest is washing!" announced Keith. Bird's Nest was code for Mrs. Ross, nicknamed for the grey hair that she piled messily in a bun. We grinned at each other and solemnly headed to the Hardings' where, if you climbed on the garage roof and laid flat on your stomach in just the right way, you could peer in the basement window and watch Mrs. Ross doing the laundry—stark naked. Feeding the wet items through the cylinders that pressed excess water out, she took the flattened fabric coils and folded them carefully in the wicker basket at her feet. Dressed, she would eventually carry the basket outside and hang the wet things on her clothesline, the pulley screeching like a murder of crows as she fed the line along, pegging items in place.

"What if her boobies get caught in the rollers?" had often been the subject of our hilarity. I would remember this years later, clad in a hospital gown, waiting for the technician to release me from acrylic plates after my first mammogram.

"At least they didn't splat out," I thought, "or grow longer and flatter."

We knew secrets and we guarded them. We knew when someone got smacked by their dad, when Mr. Gilchrist was out of work, when Mr. Vickers got drunk, and how Mrs. Eliot got her shiner. We roamed and spied as easily as we played. We acted out scenes from our favourite TV shows, pretend-shopped in the colour pages of the Eaton's catalogue, rode bikes, jumped rope, played tag and hide 'n seek, climbed TV antennas, and peeked in windows.

Mr. and Mrs. Curtin were an older couple who lived in a yellow brick house with a square hillock on their front lawn. The Curtins liked us and we sat on their hill often, favouring them with our company. Mrs. Curtin would bring us melamine cups filled with pink lemonade. When they moved away to live with their married daughter, we stood in regimental formation along their driveway and waved.

Later that week, a new family moved in, and we gawked openly as their furniture and boxes were unloaded and carried in the front door. There were two boys, one slightly younger than we were. The Smiths. They looked stuck up. The boys wore knee socks and shorts and brown leather shoes. We eyed their outfits with derision. Our own play-clothes were well worn with patched knees, carefully mended rips, and canvas sneakers.

Early one Saturday morning, we approached the Smiths' front door, ordered by our respective mothers to "be nice," and asked if the older boy would come out to play. Mrs. Smith smiled at us and said that Bradley needed to finish practicing the piano first. He was self-conscious when he joined us, loping across the lawn with stiff legs and arms, as though unaccustomed to the movements of his own body. We watched his approach with interest, as curious about him as we would be a caterpillar on tree bark or a dead baby bird.

We introduced ourselves and got to the business at hand right away.

We wanted to know what Bradley was *good at*. All of us were good at something. Tree-climbing, conkers, bike tricks, trading. He wouldn't look at us, staring down instead at his crossed legs, awkward in our circle on the grassy boulevard. "Keith's good at farting," offered Paul. "They stink like nothing you ever smelled before." We laughed and corroborated the statement, each of us trying to help establish Keith's reputation as a premium farter. "Once, he even farted in class," Paul added. "So loud, Lownie turned around and demanded to know, 'who had been so rude as to foul the air.'"

"*Foul the air!*" we snorted, enjoying the ridiculous phrase.

Bradley wasn't amused. His ears went all red and he looked like he was going to cry. We were silent, watching him. Intrigued by the flushing on his pale, clear skin. Paul pulled out his prize conker—a carefully polished chestnut with a black shoelace threaded through it. "You can have this," Paul said, "if you like conkers." The rest of sat back, watching. Bradley reached for it and examined it carefully. It was a really big chestnut. The largest any of us had ever owned.

"Thanks," he said, looking up and smiling at Paul, just briefly.

The rest of us followed suit and reached into our pockets to pull out cat-eye marbles, pieces of fools gold, coloured rabbit feet, and a few hunks of coloured glass. Keith had a pen from Niagara Falls with a *Maid of the Mist* boat that floated inside the clear shaft. By turn, all of these things were examined and exclaimed over by Bradley.

"You got anything?" I finally asked.

"Just this," he said, reaching into his pocket. "My grandpa gave it to me." Bradley took out a shiny silver dollar. We passed it around the circle and admired both sides of it before returning it. None of us had seen one before. Bradley had, with this small act, eased his way into the fringe of our group, and we agreed to afford him tag-along privileges.

There was a pecking order in our domain, and a system that dictated the way things were done. When it rained: we played in the Grants' basement. When it was hot, we played in the Clarkes' shaded yard. For dodge ball, we went to the Wilsons'. We were accustomed to piling into a neighbourhood kitchen for a group snack. "Mom, can we come in?" was the preliminary, uttered by whoever lived there. And then, permission granted, six or seven of us would crowd into the room, wash our hands at the sink, and sit at the formica table, often two bottoms per chair, while we waited.

Bradley had joined us on these forays several times before we decided that it was *his turn* to host. After carefully rehearsing the ritual, we followed him to the side door and waited for things to unfold. But Mrs. Smith did *not* invite us in. Instead, she came to the door carrying a leafy green thing and broke off pieces that she passed out, calling them "romaine hearts." It tasted like lettuce but was skimpy and pointed. We said "thank you," awkwardly and walked away in disbelief, feeling strangely embarrassed.

I scanned the wooden bins of produce with interest the next time I was at the grocery store. When my mother selected a large head of iceberg lettuce for our cart, I told her the Smith secret. "You know, Mum, the Smiths eat romaine hearts." I felt ashamed to be saying it aloud, as if I was complicit in their unconventionality.

"Hmm," responded my mother, "I suppose that's okay if it suits them."

But she had not understood what it was that I was trying to communicate: that the Smiths weren't *like us*.

All of us have grown up and left home, and the neighbourhood itself is unrecognizable. Our comfortable houses have been replaced by condominiums and a subway stop. Often, when shopping for groceries, I choose radicchio, arugula, spinach, or iceberg lettuce. I avoid the romaine with a childish loyalty to my simple understanding of life as it once was.

The Canadian Shield

WE WERE IN GRADE FOUR, sitting alphabetically by surname in straight rows. Our morning commenced after our outer clothing was hung on hooks in the respective boys' and girls' cloakrooms. The smell of our wet woollen coats and hats and mittens permeated the room. We stood at attention for the national anthem and "God Save the Queen," singing lustily for royalty we had never glimpsed but whose picture was hung at the front of the classroom, centered over the blackboard. A smiling young queen with blushing cheeks and a white satin gown billowing out around her. This was followed by the Lord's Prayer. Only then were we directed to "be seated."

On Thursdays, we began our day with Canadian Geographical Studies. It was my second least favourite subject. Mathematics was worse. I often circled the room reciting my times tables, head lowered with embarrassment. Six times around for an error in the six times table. Nine times around for an error in the nine times table. Dreading the twelve times table. Slipping down in my seat, praying that my name not be called. Mondays, Wednesdays, and Fridays, the day began with Mathematics. But on one particular Thursday morning, Miss Lowney (or "Looney Lowney" as we called her) was unusually inspired, and her lesson filled us with a deep sense of nationalism.

She began by pulling down a map of North America. For reasons I did not then understand, there were pictures of little chocolate bars floating in the oceans on all sides. These provided a terrific distraction because, although I no longer remember their names, a chocolate bar was, at that time, a substantial treat. Chocolate bars were to be shared, square by square, with everyone in the family, and the foil saved for the craft basket, to be pulled out on a "rainy day" or when we were home sick from school and relegated to long, boring hours in our beds. The foil could then be smoothed carefully over an empty matchbox, making a small, shiny container for our treasures: a shard of sea glass, a perfectly smooth pebble, a marble, a tiny wishbone. With her blond wooden pointer, Lowney banged the map and said, "Here is the Canadian Shield! Our country is built on it. Rock solid." Using her pointer, she outlined its shape and continued her lesson. The impression left was that our country was unshakeable. Stolid. Unlike California, which was prone to earthquakes that swallowed up people and houses and cities into bottomless crevices, *we* were safe.

I had many questions but no opportunity to ask them. How could a crevice be bottomless? Why wouldn't those people from California just emerge on the other side of the world? We were not encouraged to ask questions. Instead we traced the outline of our rock-solid Canadian Shield onto maps of the country, and shaded the area in pink, and the rest of the landscape in bright green. Around it, the oceans and lakes were blue. All your strokes had to go in the same direction or else it "looked liked scribbling." It was a very prescriptive activity, but it left me with an overwhelming sense of satisfaction. I was good at colouring, for one thing. And I lived in a country where I would always be safe. We would not disappear into a deep crack in the earth.

On the pavement of the girls' playground was a large map of the world in bright primary colours. At recess, we scraped away the ice and muck and studied our country. It was painted bright yellow. The Canadian Shield was not delineated. We were disappointed and tried to trace the outlines with the toes of our clumsy brown galoshes. Now that we possessed this important piece of knowledge, it was somehow important to see it. The boys played on their own side. Little wooden flags on crossed wooden bases marked the separation between the two areas. When the bell rang, we lined up in two parallel lines, twenty feet apart, and prepared to enter through the Girls' and Boys' entrances, our sexes carved into monolithic blocks over the two doorways. We were not permitted to talk to each other. Only when we were deemed "quiet young Ladies and Gentlemen" were we allowed re-entrance. Dour Mr. Morton, the principal, was always at the Boys' entrance, and any one of our teachers was at the Girls' entrance. Mr. Morton was not beyond cuffing a boy on his way through the door, and we watched out of the corners of our eyes to see which of the boys would suffer his attentions. It was usually Louie.

Louie was an Italian in a neighbourhood of mostly Scottish and English families. Italian was pronounced "Eye-tally-ian" in that place. Mr. Morton thought he was "wild." At least once a week, Mr. Morton came for him, walking up to his desk and pulling him to his feet by his ear. "Come with me, young man, and I will teach you your manners," was the inevitable enjoinder. It was never clear why Louie needed manners taught, or what he had done to require such teaching. With the classroom door open, and also the office door nearby, we would wait for the loud howling and the thwack of the strap, counting the beats silently ... *eight-nine-ten* ... until it was over. Louie would return shortly and grin at those of us who dared to look at him. I walked home at lunch, as we all did back then, and Louie was often in front of or just behind me. I asked him if it hurt to get the strap. "Not so much," was his response. He had accepted that this was his lot in school, as it was mine to have to circle the room reciting my times tables.

When my parents asked, "How was school today?" I would report, "Louie got the strap again." I was too humiliated to tell them about my regular marches around the room.

Louie was not the only one who got strapped. Stephan did too. Stephan was Greek and his name was pronounced Steven but it was spelled funny. He had a sister, Mary, and she was in Grade Three. Stephan didn't get the strap at school; he got it at home. Stephan sometimes came into our classroom, slumped down into his chair, put his head on his arms, and cried. We weren't allowed to sit down until Miss Lowney invited us, but she never said anything to Stephan. She didn't make him stand when he was crying. A couple of times, his cotton shirt was stuck to his back with bloody streaks. We were all scared when we saw that. Miss Lowney went to get the school nurse and Mr. Morton. But nothing ever happened. Maybe Mr. Morton thought he just plain deserved it. We all liked Stephan. Sometimes he crossed into the girls' playground to find his sister. Then he would open his coat and Mary would snuggle against him and they would hug, and he would pat her gently, like an adult. Nobody ever told.

Driving up north that summer, I noticed, for the first time, the walls of granite that towered above the highway. Miles of sharp-edged rock face on either side of the busy road. "Yeah," said my father, "they dynamited to put the road through. Crews spent years drillin' and blowin' the rock to smithereens. Then they brought in big machines and cleaned up the mess to put in the road." He was pleased with this. A tidy explanation of the passageway channelled through our security. A substantial proof of diligence and hard work.

But I was not satisfied. They had created a weakness.

"Why didn't they just put the road *over* it, Dad?"

"Cost too much. Cheaper this way."

I was silent with the enormity of what had been done.

We always picnicked on a big outcrop by Devil's Wishbone. I sat there one afternoon, scratching at the lichen with my fingernail. Scraping up the brittle growths and turning them over. Circular, coarse little mats of grey and brown and white lace adhering to the rock. Small pads of moss in the deeper indentations. Occasional wildflowers and scrawny weeds growing in the shallow soil that filled the crevices. Life clinging to, and softening, the ancient, weathered mass. I felt safe there in the hot sun, the lake lapping quietly against the base of our boulder. Around me, rocks sloped into the water and disappeared from sight into the lake bottom.

The lake itself was deep and black. "Almost two-hun'ered feet in the middle," said my father. He tried teaching me to swim there once—abruptly tossing me in and expecting me to splash my way to safety. Instead I sank, shocked and indignant, my eyes closed tight against the cold. He hoisted me out by the straps on my bathing suit. Unapologetic. My fingernails were filled with light, gritty sand that I had scratched up from the bottom. It was an experiment not to be repeated, and I crept back from the shoreline distrustfully on all other occasions.

Divers found a wagon in the lake one summer, and there were plans made to wrap it with chains and pull it from its resting place. Line drawings were printed in the paper. Someone did the research and discovered that a young woman and her ten-year-old son had drowned in the lake one night in the winter of 1860. She was taking a short cut home across the ice with two horses when they all broke through and disappeared. People on the shoreline saw her lantern fade unexpectedly. The locals were sure that the wagon should be retrieved for the nearby Pioneer Museum.

I wondered if the woman felt as I had: startled to find herself immersed in the chill water, panicked, and unable to open her eyes, fill her lungs with air, or regulate her movements. Had she reached for her son and clung to him as their winter clothing pulled them downward, or had they attempted to grab at thin shards of ice that broke away as they struggled? Had she felt cradled by the rocks and cushioned by the shallow sandy covering? Was it a peaceful ending or was it terror-filled? These thoughts preoccupied me. Worried me.

On a low bookshelf in the small rented cottage were discarded games in shabby boxes with pieces missing—like the Monopoly board without any money or cards but with many little green plastic houses and red hotels. There were also some schoolbooks. Among them was *Pirates and Pathfinders*, a musty text that we still used at Willow Lane Public School. When I was in danger of becoming "underfoot" or "bored," my mother would pass it to me, admonishing me to "go outside and improve yourself." Having set this course for me, she would later follow up on my study by quizzing me disinterestedly.

"Tell me what you learned," she would prompt, while busily setting cutlery and plates down on the plastic tablecloth. I would, in turn, sometimes retaliate by testing her—inventing a phony explorer and subjecting them to a violent and gruesome death. If I enjoyed the telling too much, she would look at me sharply and challenge my fabrication. "Your stories are better than the ones in the book," she would say. And we would both of us smile, happy with our comfortable ritual.

I remember that day when my father dropped me into the lake, and how, while I struggled to catch my breath, I saw on his face the briefest flash of disappointment, a momentary glimpse of something unspoken that filled me with shame for having failed to float upwards.

Creamers

THERE WERE FIFTY-THREE CREAMERS in the collection. She counted them periodically. Obsessively cataloguing her small family.

Antique Jaeger & Co J&C Louise Bavaria Creamer, mint condition. Porcelain with exquisite soft hand-painted roses. Gold trim. 3.75 inches tall x 3 inches wide. Circa 1910. Excellent condition.

This one she called Gladys. Gladys mostly spoke to her when she was in the small garden out back. Made her crush the emptied eggshells and spread them around the roses. Gladys could be extremely intrusive. She had an opinion about everything. Insisted that she would make tea in the Brown Betty and not just dunk a bag in a mug. You got more tea that way. There was no waste. And it was civilized. How things were meant to be done. Joan often grew weary of Gladys. Joan was alone and not quite so particular as Gladys would wish. It had been a long time since Joan had had to shut the bathroom door or dress and undress in the bedroom. She could strip off in the laundry room if she wanted, and cross the house in her bra and underpants if she felt like it. There was no one to see. No one to *tsk* at her. No one to reach for her suddenly to caress the small of her back, or comment on the gentle sags now visible. No one but Gladys, that is. And the others, of course.

Joan marshalled the entire inventory on her dining room table. They had started on the kitchen windowsill, spread to the tea table, filled her mantle piece, and gradually migrated to the polished cherry surface. An ecru lace cloth was draped gracefully across the surface, its points hanging artfully down in long tapered folds. The creamers were aligned in regimental formation. Handles pointing south, spouts pointing north. They were dusted on Wednesdays. Washed, one row only, on successive Fridays. Scalding hot water with just a drop of bleach. Mary, in particular, disliked the bleach.

Vintage Royal Bayreuth Bird Creamer. Excellent condition. No chips or cracks. No staining. Sweet piece. 4 inches high x 4.5 inches handle to spout. Vintage. Early 1900s.

Mary looked like a baby Robin. The name suited her. It just came to Joan one day. She saw her in the antique store and thought, that creamer was owned by a woman named Mary. And so she bought it, took it home for the collection, and called it Mary. Speculating about Mary had provided a diversion for Joan. She imagined a whole life for Mary—a husband, a house, and a son. She imagined Mary with child, longing for a daughter. A girl to read with and play house with. To teach to bake. But the girl, when she was born, was damaged. Addled. Mentally retarded is what they said back then. It broke Mary's heart. But she had the creamer and a matching sugar bowl and she made tea for the girl anyway, chirping as she poured milk from the tiny bird-like spout. Pretending to be the chirping Robin. Trying to engage her. Make her smile. But the girl did not respond. Instead she waved her hands spastically, knocking over the tea cup and sugar bowl, spilling cookies onto the floor. Mary's daughter was just like Elaine, a heartbreak. Fortunately there was Alice, the practical Alice.

Vintage green Depression glass. Footed. Approximately 3-3/4 inches tall x 3-1/2 inches wide. Distributed free in boxed food items. 1930s. No chips, cracks, or scratches. Smooth seam. Estate sale.

The others sometimes thought Alice was a piece of work. But Joan liked her. In fact, Joan thought she sounded a little like her mother. Alice was the one Joan turned to when she needed some stiffening up. Some encouragement. She had an unending catalogue of expressions. *In for a penny, in for a pound. No use crying over spilt milk. A whistling girl and a crowing hen always come to bad end. Never give the devil a ride; he will always want to drive. Kindness costs nothing. If something sounds too good to be true, it probably is. A person who never made a mistake, has never done anything. Necessity is the mother of invention. A person is known by the company they keep. Don't make a mountain out of a molehill.* And so forth. Occasionally however, she did grate. On all of them. In fact, some days, Joan actually had to remove Alice from her place in line and set her over on the sideboard. Just to keep her subdued.

Richard had been gone a long time now. Apart far longer than they had been together. How she missed his bright red coat. A scarlet satin ballgown, chosen to complement the red officer's jacket, was still encased in plastic at the back of her closet. She wore it the night he proposed. Just before he shipped out for his first assignment. They married quickly when he returned, both of them eager for a *full joining together* before he left again. Alice understood their lust. The practicality of such hurried arrangements. *You've made your bed, now you'll have to lie in it.*

The creamers were arranged according to their country of origin—France, Czechoslovakia, Bavaria, Germany, England, America—and further arranged by size and colour. Joan had deliberated grouping them by style, but found the struggles overwhelming. Alice, for instance, refused to stand near Grace, who she claimed was *not really, not technically, depression glass*. She was right, of course, but her remarks were offensive to the gentle Grace.

Vintage Bubble Glass Footed Depression-era Creamer. 3-5/8 inches tall. 3-1/4 inches outside diameter. Bottom seam has extra roughness. Small scratch near the spout. Manufactured 1940. Pale pink.

Grace was lovely. Full of surprises. The bubbles would sometimes catch the light and reflect a tiny prism of colour. Delicate despite the softened orb shape. And Grace could always be counted on for a sweet whisper of encouragement. *You've still got great legs.* These sorts of things mattered now that there was no one else to notice.

After Richard left, Joan had concentrated all of her energy on Elaine. Determined to coddle her. Ensure that she was not damaged by the separation. The empty house. Furniture half gone. Velvet drapes and mother-in-law's Limoges removed. Elaine did not notice these things. Focused only on words, books, and television. French. Italian. Languages. They came easily to her. She listened to language tapes and watched movies with subtitles. English was common. Inferior. She pretended to be displaced. The child of a diplomat, warehoused in Ottawa, residing with a Canadian foster-mother. She told the school counsellor that her true identity could not be revealed for reasons of *international security*. They believed her. Joan indulged her and did not dispute the stories. The fabricated life. But it was only the beginning.

Breaches with reality. That's what they told her at the hospital. Your daughter has breaches with reality. *Was this wrong?* Joan wondered. Now, in retrospect, she thought that she understood. Grace continued to try to explain it to her. *She can't cope with reality if she doesn't know what's really real.* Really? Joan wondered.

Fraureuth Peach luster creamer. Mother of pearl interior. Circa 1860s. Measures 4-1/4 inches x 4-3/4 inches. Good condition. No staining. Some crazing.

Crazing. How wonderful. Joan believed that a woman named Elsye had owned this creamer. And Elsye, too, was a little crazed. How else did one cope with all that was required? Joan had purchased this creamer at the antique market near the Glebe. It was a dreary day and she needed a distraction. Elaine was, once again, in treatment. This meant a weekly supervised visit to the Institute. She hadn't bothered to tell Richard, this time. "Keep me informed," was his last order. But he was preoccupied with his "new" family. A ten-year-old son. An heir. A legacy. The son would do what Elaine could not. Follow Richard into the Academy and join the rugby team. Win the same honours that Richard, and his father before him, had won. A dynasty of military rugby types in red dress uniforms. Elsye understood this. Understood what it was like to lie under the covers at night and feel an aching for something. Elsye's husband had died young. An outbreak of something. Influenza likely. He was just thirty. She lost everything. Had to return home to her father's house a widow. She hated the pity of it. Joan understood that. *The pity.* She had been pitied. Richard had left and she did not know the why of it. One night they were together in bed, whispering, hands held; the next night he was gone. In between was a mystery. He woke, packed for an assignment, and never returned. A phone call several weeks later. *A coward*, is what Elsye called him. *Not man enough to face her. To say goodbye.* But he was an officer. Highly respected. In charge of one hundred and seventy men. How could that be?

Vintage masons Ironstone Red Vista Creamer. 1825. Crown marking. 4-1/4 inches tall x 4-1/2 inches wide spout to handle. No cracks, chips or repairs.

This was among Joan's favourites. A couple walking arm-in-arm in front of an old gothic-windowed country house, a small child and dog close by. A family captured. This creamer was called Sara. Sara was the lady in the picture. Sara was also the lady who owned the creamer. Joan was sure of it. It must have been part of the breakfast set. It was not fine enough for a formal tea set. Ironstone was only used by the family for family meals, and only for breakfast and luncheon. Dinner would always be served on china. Sara would preside over the breakfast room, pouring tea, passing the biscuits and sausages, plates of dry toast. Her husband, William, would eat quickly, not lingering for small talk. Eager to begin his day in the city.

The help would clear. Sara would retire to her sitting room. The children would be brought to her.

Elaine would be brought to Joan. Seated on an orange vinyl settee, Joan would flip through shabby magazines, waiting for Elaine. A nurse would walk with her, holding her elbow, steering her gently. "Say hello to your mother," she would prompt. Elaine would look at her, eyes liquid and unfocused. Joan would press into her hands a gift. A token. A German dictionary. A pink cardigan. New shoes. Elaine would hold these things closely. Attempting to assimilate. And the nurse would return. Taking Elaine from the room but not from her. She had already gone.

Suzette's Garden

SUZETTE WAS THIRTEEN WHEN SHE STARTED her first garden. It was during the summer she spent with her grandmother in Montreal. Her grandfather had died that winter, and, in an effort to appease her own sense of guilt for not having done more to help, Suzette's mother had packed her off with her summer clothes on only her second journey alone. No discussion went into this unilateral decision. No consideration for the plans that Suzette had already made with her best friends, plans that involved long days sunning themselves in their back yards, straps pulled down on their bathing suits, bottles of baby oil at the ready for slathering their baking bodies, and plant misters filled with water to cool them down. Plans that involved spying on the neighbourhood boys and watching them do shirtless stunts on their boards. But these plans were crushed when Suzette realized that she was powerless to change the course of her summer, and that her determined mother, an agent for an insurance company, was not about to alter the arrangements already set in motion. Grandfather was dead. Gran was lonely. Mother was busy. It was a perfect blending of the elements coming together. They went together to Union Station to catch the train.

Arriving in Montreal in the early evening, Suzette did as she had been instructed and took a taxi to Gran's house. Her mother had carefully printed out the address on an office index card, and Suzette unfolded this from her wallet and passed it to the taxi driver through the window. He nodded at her and opened the trunk, placing her large backpack and small overnight bag inside. Suzette kept her purse, artfully and safely slung across her right shoulder, resting upon the flat of her left hip. Holding the strap secure, she climbed into the back of the cab and settled herself. She held the twenty-dollar bill her mother had given her to pay the fare tightly in her palm. It was a short ride, and when the taxi stopped in front of her gran's house—grey slate, with an ornate roof spiked with large gables and decorative iron trim, window frames painted in a brilliant pink, and a shiny black front door—Suzette passed the driver the money and prepared to slide out. Pulling a knob on the dash, the driver popped open the trunk, and then came around to her door and held it open. She felt transformed, having a man hold a door open for her. She emerged from the cab gracefully, her foot carefully pointed as she had seen Hollywood actresses do when exiting limousines prior to walks along red carpets.

Feeling independent and suddenly sophisticated, Suzette thanked the driver with self-conscious French, "*Merci, Monsieur,*" and walked up the short path to her gran's front door. Gran was standing there waiting, arms extended for a hearty embrace. "*Ma petite,*" said Gran, "I am so happy to have you here."

Entering the house, Suzette was immediately overcome by a sense of sorrow. The house was in mourning, with panels of black cotton fabric draping the hall mirror and several large pictures in the living room. A large framed photograph of her grandfather had been set up in the middle of the dining room table, which was now pushed up against the wall with chairs lined up to face it in a curious shrine-like arrangement. The picture was surrounded by a tidy row of red glass votive candles, which were lit and flickering with faint darts of flame. Gran was dressed in a plain black dress and heavy black stockings. She looked hot and oddly unfamiliar. Suzette was accustomed to Gran in more colourful outfits that expressed her sense of style: bold flowers or bright stripes. The plain black was unattractive. Suzette no longer felt like a Hollywood starlet beginning a summer adventure, but instead felt as though she were trapped somewhere that was no longer familiar. This was not going to be any fun.

Unpacking her things in the small guest room, Suzette began to compose in her head the text she would send her best friend, Evelyn. "Can't imagine how awful. Bored. Depressing. I want to die." Suzette imagined Evelyn reading the text in her pale green bedroom, lying on her bed, experimenting with eye shadow, and then rubbing it off with toilet paper before leaving her room. Painting her toenails. Checking her underarms for hair growth.

Suzette thought about these things while filling the two drawers in the dresser that Gran had emptied. Piling her toiletries and contraband cosmetics on the bed, she picked up a tube of lipstick—a cast off she had been given by Evelyn's older sister, Janelle—and applied a light coating of Pink Passion to her lower lip. Smooching her lips together as she had seen Janelle do, she went back down the stairs to join her gran.

"*Mon dieu*," said Gran, "You look so pretty."

"Thank you, Gran," said Suzette, somewhat guiltily. "I only wear it sometimes."

"A woman should never be without her lipstick," said Gran, smiling at her.

Suzette forgot, during the course of the next few hours, that she was supposed to be dying of boredom. Gran had stocked the fridge with Suzette's favourite treats, and dinner that night consisted of fish sticks, brownies, apple pie, and Coke. Gran ate exactly what Suzette selected and the two of them carried their plates to the kitchen table where they nibbled their meals together.

"*Ma petite*," said Gran, as the light faded and the sky grew dark, "you must be tired after your journey. Let us go to bed and dream sweet dreams." Gran reached out her hand for

Suzette's, and they left their plates in the sink and climbed the steep carpeted stairs to the bedrooms.

Suzette was tired when she slipped into bed, and the only text she managed was to her mother. "Here safe," she said. "XO." Suzette had slept alone in this room once before. That was the time following her father's car accident five years ago, when he was in the hospital. She had been in the way then, and her mother had sent her to her grandparents' for a visit while her father recuperated. But he had not, as her mother had promised, recovered, and she was driven to Toronto in the backseat of her grandfather's large black car for the funeral. Her grandparents stayed with them for a couple of weeks, but her mother said she needed to "establish new routines" and indicated, far too soon, when it was time for them to leave.

Suzette was angry when they left. Angry that she had been left alone with this woman who resembled her mother but was completely different from her, and angry that no one was left in the house who would pull her into their arms and hug her tightly. She missed her father's softening presence. Her mother was obsessed with the lawsuit and preoccupied by court dates and bills. Years later, when they finally won a settlement, there was no joy in the victory. It was simply "what we are owed," according to her mother.

Suzette thought of these things while she drifted off to sleep, but she slept easily. She felt safe in this house, and she dreamed of her father and her grandfather and their shared love of sweet things. In her dream, they were making ice-cream sundaes with large soup bowls filled with corn syrup and vanilla ice cream, and walnuts and maraschino cherries, and chocolate sauce. Suzette woke refreshed and made her way to the small upstairs bathroom for a quick shower. After pulling a comb through her wet hair and dressing hastily in shorts and a T-shirt, she bounced down the stairs to find that Gran was already in the kitchen mixing a huge bowl of waffle batter.

"*Bonjour, ma petite. Comment vas-tu?*"

"I dreamed of Dad and Grandpa last night," replied Suzette, kissing her grandmother on the cheek. "They were making sundaes."

"Ah, yes," smiled Gran, "They both liked sweets."

Suzette reached across the kitchen counter and picked out a couple of very plump blueberries from the white porcelain bowl. Gran smiled at her and nodded her head, as if to say, "go ahead, that's what they're there for." Suzette loved that about Gran—everything was always all right.

Gran had dressed in a black dress again, but it was mostly covered by a brilliant pink apron with large pink tulips sprayed all over in a wild pattern. "I like your apron, Gran," offered Suzette.

"*Merci*, Suzette," replied Gran, smiling broadly, "I love pink tulips."

The waffles were soon ready, and Suzette and Gran sat down at the kitchen table. Gran was not like her mother, picking at food and counting calories. Gran believed that good food was meant to be enjoyed. Her figure demonstrated this; she was well rounded and very soft for hugging. This was something else Suzette appreciated.

"Did you call your *Maman* last night?" asked Gran, "before bed?"

"Yes," said Suzette, "I texted her."

"What is texting her?" asked Gran gently. "I don't know that."

"Here, I'll show you," said Suzette, pulling her pink cell phone from her shorts' pocket. Opening it, she scrolled through the text messages, until she found one from her mother, "Be careful and let me know when you arrive. Mom."

"See," said Suzette, "this is how we communicate."

"You don't talk on that phone?" asked her grandmother, looking a little sceptical.

"Not always," said Suzette. "It's cheaper; we have a plan."

"What is the plan?" enquired Gran.

"It's this monthly thing, it lets me send and receive unlimited texts each month, but I only get twenty minutes real talk time, and that goes fast when it's long distance."

"Oh," responded Gran, "I see." She took in this information carefully and processed it while collecting the dirty dishes from the table. "And your *Maman* does this too?" she probed.

"Yes, Gran," laughed Suzette. "*Maman* does this too. Would you like to try one?"

"No, *ma petite,* I don't think so. I like to *talk* on the telephone."

Suzette smiled at Gran and watched her while she rinsed the dirty dishes under the tap. "Do you want me to help wash?" she asked.

"No, *ma petite,*" said Gran, smiling at her. "You are my guest today."

"What are we going to do?" asked Suzette. "Do you know?"

"I do," smiled Gran. "Today we are going to go shopping on Rue Sherbrooke and I will buy you any one thing that you want. And then we will have a nice lunch and maybe do more shopping. How does that sound?"

"Awesome," said Suzette, getting up from her chair and hugging her grandmother tightly around the waist. "It sounds great!"

Gran wrapped her arms around Suzette and kissed the top of her head. Suzette inhaled the scent of her—lavender water and waffle batter—and grinned. She had forgotten how much fun her grandmother could be. Gran washed her hands, removed her pink apron, and tucked some stray wisps of hair behind her ears before locating the house key and her black leather handbag. This she hooked on her arm, which she linked with Suzette's, and together they locked the front door and headed downtown. Gran was accustomed to walking everywhere, and she maintained a good pace with Suzette. They nodded at several neighbours and greeted one or two more as they navigated their way to Rue Sherbrooke.

"I think," said Gran, as they descended the escalator to the underground concourse, "that you should decide which store we go into first." Suzette smiled at this and skipped though the glass doors and into the large marble hallway. "Would you like a new outfit?" Gran enquired, "or something for your room, perhaps?"

"I'm not sure," answered Suzette, considering the options carefully. "Maybe we could just look first?"

"Of course we can," agreed Gran. "That's a good idea."

The first boutique they went into had very modern and very stylish fashions. The skirts were gathered at their sides by small chains that hung from their waistbands. The hems were uneven and the skirts cut very full. Suzette thought that they looked very chic and wanted to try one on, but the colours were drab and depressing—charcoal grey and a muddy mauve. "It might be hard," remarked Gran, "to find a top that matches this nicely."

"Yes," said Suzette, agreeably, "I think you're right."

They smiled at each other and went to the next boutique where a display of summer T-shirts attracted Suzette. The T-shirts were fabricated with a light gauzy overlay that had been slashed to reveal the cotton T-shirt underneath. The shoulders were studded with rhinestones, and there was a flounce of lace along the bottom hem. "A lot of work went into these," remarked Gran. "I think they are very stylish."

"Yes," agreed Suzette, "but the colours aren't very nice." The T-shirts were in unusual colour combinations of pink gauze with grey cotton, or black gauze with olive green cotton, or brown gauze with black cotton.

"Perhaps we can find some brighter colours in another store," suggested Gran. "Shall we look?"

And so Suzette and her grandmother walked through the concourse, perusing the inventory of all of the boutiques, looking for something really stylish and chic. Gran was very patient with Suzette and never once suggested that her choices were eccentric or impractical. Neither did she complain about the cost of the clothing. Suzette knew that her mother would refuse to pay thirty-five dollars for a T-shirt with rips in it, or sixty dollars for a skirt with an uneven hem and chains that would get caught in the washing machine. "I love you, Gran," she said spontaneously.

"Bless you, *ma petite*. I love you too," responded her Gran.

They had lunch at a crêperie, and ordered sweet crêpes with mounds of whipped cream. Gran ordered exactly the same thing as Suzette, and they dug into their lunches with mutual enjoyment. When they had finished eating, Gran ordered a cup of tea, and she sipped at it while Suzette had a milkshake.

"Mom never lets me have milkshakes," confessed Suzette. "She thinks I'll get fat."

"You are still a growing girl," said Gran, smiling at Suzette. "There is time later to worry about your figure. Milk is good for your bones."

After they paid their bill, they walked through the concourse one more time, looking for an outfit. There was nothing that Suzette thought was "just right," and she was unwilling to squander this one chance at getting exactly what she wanted.

"I am sorry, *ma petite*," said Gran, "that there was nothing here for you. Perhaps we should try another day?"

"I'm sorry too," said Suzette. "I've made you tired from all the walking."

"Not at all," said Gran. "It gave me great pleasure."

Arm in arm, the two of them retraced their steps and began their walk back to Gran's house. "Do you miss Grandpa a lot?" asked Suzette.

"Yes, *ma petite,* all the time. I forget sometimes that he is gone, and I go into a room and expect him to be there," replied Gran.

"Me too," said Suzette. "I really miss my dad. Mom is always witchy now. She's too busy working to have any fun, and she always nags me."

"She loved your father very much, *ma petite*. A woman doesn't recover from such a loss."

"Well, you lost Grandpa and you're not witchy," responded Suzette.

"Your grandfather had a good life, *ma petite*. A long and happy life. It was his time. Your father was much too young to die, and your mother is much too young to be so much alone."

They walked in silence for a few minutes. Suzette watched her feet and tried to step down on them ball first, like a dancer, instead of slapping them down on the sidewalk. She concentrated on this, gliding awkwardly beside her gran, intent on looking graceful.

"You are very quiet, *ma petite*," her grandmother began. "Perhaps we should take a detour on our way home and go to the park?"

"That's all right with me," said Suzette, still gliding, "but won't you get too tired from the walking?"

"*Non*, not at all" smiled Gran. "We will ride." While walking, they had been passed several times by horse-drawn carriages. These were for the tourists, and the horses were decorated with garlands of silk flowers and long brightly coloured ribbons. Suzette had never been for a ride in one of these before, had never considered what it might feel like to be elevated in a carriage, parading through the streets and park.

Gran directed Suzette to a bench on the opposite side of the street, and they crossed carefully, avoiding the oncoming traffic and pedestrians. They waited only a few minutes before a horse and carriage pulled up, and the driver greeted Gran, cheerfully, "*Aimeriez-vous faire un tour en voiture, Madame?*"

"*Oui, Monsieur*," agreed Gran, rising and smiling broadly. Suzette climbed in after Gran, and the two of them sat together snugly on the seat. "To the park, please," instructed Gran.

The driver nodded his head and clicked his tongue at the horses. They set off at a leisurely pace down the avenue and across to the park. Suzette could not help but notice that Gran was enjoying herself thoroughly, waving at the tourists in other carriages and smiling at passersby.

"This is how the Queen waves, Suzette," said Gran, demonstrating a pivoting wrist action with a static arm and elbow. "Let's do it!" And, giggling, Suzette pivoted her wrist on the left side of the carriage, while Gran pivoted her wrist on the right side of the carriage. The driver looked back at them, over his shoulder, and laughed at them good-naturedly. He took them on a complete circuit of the park before finally pulling over at a bench and helping them to dismount.

"That was very pleasant," said Gran to the driver while she paid him. "*En effet, très agréable.*"

"*Merci, Monsieur,*" echoed Suzette, climbing down from the carriage to join her gran.

They watched him round a corner before looking at each other and smiling.

"Let us go to the pond," said Gran. "Your grandfather loved to watch the ducks in the pond. And there is a beautiful garden there as well."

Nodding in agreement, Suzette linked her arm in her gran's, and they walked along the cobbled pathway to the pond. A large garden was in flower, and Suzette again forgot herself, taking delight in the bright pinks and blues that were blooming there. "Look, Gran," she called, "these pink tulips are like your apron!"

Gran came close to look at them and smiled at her granddaughter. "Yes, you are right, *ma petite*, they are very like."

"They're pretty!" said Suzette agreeably. "I think they're my favourite flower."

"Why then, we should plant some," Gran said, smiling at her. "Let us make our own garden and fill it with pink tulips!"

"And maybe some of these blue things?" asked Suzette, pointing out a bright blue wispy plant.

"*Absolument!*" agreed her gran.

Gran's house was not very far from the park, and they walked home slowly, savouring the late afternoon. Both of them were a little weary from their day, and they did not eat dinner. Instead, they sat on the front steps, and Gran picked up her crocheting while Suzette read her text messages, and sent a couple of brief updates to her mom and her friends. These were non-committal texts, revealing a little of the excitement of the day, but also maintaining some sense of mystique: "went shopping in Rue Sherbrooke, saw amazing new fashions." They retired early. Suzette slept well and did not rise until much later than usual.

Gran was sitting at the kitchen table flipping through magazines when Suzette went downstairs to greet her. She was embarrassed to see that it was nearly ten a.m. "*Bonjour, ma petite,*" Gran greeted her. "*Comment vas-tu?*"

Suzette moved closer to her grandmother and draped herself around the older woman, hugging her tightly. They remained locked together in their embrace until Suzette began to worry that the hug was hurting her grandmother by forcing her to bend in an unnatural position. "Are you okay, Gran?" asked Suzette, stepping back and freeing herself.

"But of course," laughed Gran, "who wouldn't be after such a hug? When you are old, Suzette, you cherish the times when people remember to touch you."

"Mom doesn't like hugs anymore," replied Suzette confidentially. "They make her back stiff."

"Your *Maman* has maybe forgotten a little what it is like to feel loved, *ma petite*. You must hug her often. Every day. And when you do this, you must squeeze your love into her with a tight, tight hug."

While her gran was speaking, Suzette had gone to the fridge and helped herself to a large bowl of raspberries. Raspberries were among her favourite fruits, and Gran had washed these and readied them for her breakfast. Suzette began to pop them into her mouth and crush them slowly with her tongue before swallowing. The burst of cold raspberry was delicious. Gran watched her and smiled.

"I have a surprise for you, *ma petite,*" said Gran. "Look out the front window."

SUZETTE'S GARDEN

Suzette got up from the kitchen chair and walked to the living room where she could look outside to the front of the house. Two men were busy stripping sod from the small patches of lawn, and a large pile of black earth was piled on tarps nearby. The whole of the yard was being removed, leaving only the ornate wrought iron stairs that descended gracefully from the front door. "Gran, what are they doing to your grass?" asked Suzette. "They're digging it all up."

Gran had entered the room behind her, and stood nearby with one hand on Suzette's shoulder. Suzette noted the brown spots that dotted the back of the hand, as well as the raised veins and knobby bits that seemed to protrude in defined ways she had not noticed before. The hand was elegantly manicured, with soft pink nail polish and large diamond rings. The skin was smooth and cool. It was the hand of an old lady, thought Suzette. In an impulsive gesture, Suzette clasped the hand in her own and brought it to her lips and kissed it. Gran smiled at her but did not reference the kiss. Instead, she addressed the initial question Suzette had asked of her. "A garden, *ma petite*," she announced. "These men are going to help us plant a garden. With pink tulips and blue spider wort and anything else you want."

"For real, Gran?"

"Yes, *ma petite*, for real. I am an old woman, and I can do whatever I want. So, will you come to the nursery? We need to pick out our flowers."

Suzette and her grandmother took a taxi to Maison Hogue, where they purchased pink and blue Hydrangea bushes, pink Angeligue tulips, blue Spider Wort, Russian Sage, Midnight Blue Delphinium, Echinacea, Columbine, and Lupines.

When they were done with their selections and Gran had paid for them, the manager agreed to have everything delivered to the house the next morning. He gave them a planting guide, which they studied in the taxi on the way home.

"We should make a plan," said Gran, "and draw out where

we want to put everything—the tall ones and the short ones."

"Yes," agreed Suzette.

"*Ma petite*," smiled Gran. "Will you plan this for us when we get home?"

"*Absolument!*" said Suzette.

Gran spent the afternoon watching some television and speaking with friends on the telephone. Suzette drew garden plans at the kitchen table and coloured patches of garden with the pencil crayons that Gran had produced from a desk drawer. Suzette's garden was mostly pink and blue, and it included all of the flowers and bulbs that she could remember purchasing with her Gran. "Do you think we have enough to start with?" she asked when Gran came into the kitchen to look over her plans. "This is a very big garden."

"It will be a start, *ma petite,* and, if we need more, we will simply call up the nice man at Masion Hogue and order more. It will be fine."

They spent their night in joyful anticipation of the morning activities. Several times, Suzette walked outside to pace out the dark squares of garden that the men had excavated. She was sure that their garden would be more beautiful than any she had ever seen. Gran seemed delighted with her garden drawing and confident that their work would be much admired.

Suzette woke early and texted her mother. The text was short: "Lots to do. Making a garden. Lol." Details could come later. She scanned her incoming texts quickly and decided that there was nothing that couldn't wait until evening. When she went downstairs, she saw at once that Gran had abandoned the horrible black dress and was wearing one of her summer dresses with bright blue and red poppies.

"I thought I should wear flowers today," said Gran, smiling at her.

They ate breakfast quickly, and went outside to sort through the bags of bulbs, piles of plants, and all the small flowering bushes that had been delivered. Suzette had her garden plan in hand and kept consulting it in an attempt to organize their work. Gran sat on the iron steps and watched while Suzette carried the pots and the bags of bulbs to their various places. When everything had been placed, Gran connected the garden hose and they began to plant together. Suzette would dig the hole; Gran would fill it with water. Suzette would tip in the plant and tamp in the displaced earth, and they would move on to the next planting. In this way, Gran could mostly stand and did not have to kneel down for any length of time. They worked in this way for several hours. Many passersby stopped to speak with them and to compliment them on their work.

Suzette was excited. Gran was letting her make something beautiful without any rules. There were eighteen bags of pink tulips, since they had bought two bags each of every kind they could find. These took the longest to plant. Suzette wanted them in straight rows, like soldiers, along the edge. When all of the other plants were planted, Suzette finished the work by planting the tulips. It took her all afternoon. Gran sat on the steps and watched her. "You are a very good gardener, *ma petite*," she called out. "You have patience and gentleness. Both are needed to make a beautiful garden." Suzette glowed with the compliment. In response, she became more careful when handling the bulbs, and gentler yet when she placed them deep into the earth and covered them lovingly. She wanted Gran to see that she was right to trust her with this task.

Suzette's visit with her grandmother lasted three weeks, after which it was time to return to Toronto. She had relaxed into Gran's indulgent routines, and she realized that she would be sorry to leave her here alone in Montreal. She texted home one night, and suggested that Gran should come to visit them in Toronto. Her mother's response had been definitive: "Don't be silly. Her friends and doctors are there. She wouldn't want to."

On Suzette's last night in Montreal, Gran came into the bedroom and passed her a large paper shopping bag. "We did not find you a present, *ma petite,"* said Gran, smiling at her. "I hope this will be something you will like for school." Wrapped in tissue was one of the stylish skirts that Suzette had seen when she first arrived. It was a muddy mauve colour with silver chains looping up the sides. Also packaged in the tissue was a cotton T-shirt in black with brown gauze slashed stylishly across the body.

"Oh, Gran," exclaimed Suzette, "these are great. Thank you so much!"

"Well, *ma petite*," said Gran, sitting on the bed beside her, "we did not much like the colours at first, but then I decided that with our beautiful garden, we had created enough colour to make both of us happy for a long time. And also, I bought you this."

Gran passed her a smaller bag with Lancome written on the side. Inside were a tray of eye shadows, mascara, pink lipstick, lip liner, blush, and a set of makeup brushes. "I thought you needed some good makeup for your colouring, *ma petite*. You are a very lovely girl and need to wear the right makeup."

Suzette threw her arms around her grandmother and began to sob. Gran held her tightly for a long time. Parting in the morning was difficult. Gran was wearing her black dress again, but with Suzette's favourite apron. They ate raspberries with whipped cream for breakfast and had only a few minutes to embrace while the taxi waited. Suzette looked back and saw that her gran was waving like the Queen of England.

At home, her mom seemed relieved to hear that the journey was safe and that no one had accosted her. The outfit was taken out and examined but not particularly admired. The makeup was declared to be extravagant. Suzette looked at her mother and fought back tears. Instead of crying or running to her room, Suzette walked up to her and hugged her hard, squeezing in love.

The Marzipan Fruit Basket

THE TRAIN SEEMED VERY LARGE. The steel steps were high and I had to strain to climb them. My mother was busy with our tickets and didn't see me struggling. She was in a funny mood. I had never seen her like this. She was excited but also thoughtful. A thinking rather than talking mood. *Oma* had given me a marzipan fruit basket for the train ride, and *Opa* had passed me a paper bag filled with flower-shaped sugar fondant. This was more candy than I had ever been given in my life. I set Chatty Cathy down beside me on the seat, and began to unwrap the basket. My mother reached over and casually flipped down a small table so that I would have a surface to work on.

Inside the basket were beautifully shaped miniature fruits nestled on paper straw. Each one of them was different from the others. There was an apple, a pear, a banana, an orange, and a whole group of fruits I could not identify with certainty. I poked at them in turn, wanting to name them. My mother was not paying attention, although she didn't actually seem to be doing anything. When I asked her if I had a peach, she seemed annoyed, as though I had interrupted her. She was wearing a suit—a *pak*—in an unpleasant eggplant colour with a matching hat made with a circlet of the same eggplant material and lots of curled little feathers. I had stroked the feathers with one finger when it was on the bed in the morning, and she had snatched the hat from me and told me to be careful. It was not like her to snap at me. I asked her which one I should eat first: the orange or the apple? Which one would make a better breakfast?

"I don't care," she said, "just don't eat them all at once." I picked up the orange; it was dimpled and painted with exquisite detail. A half-inch big. I took a small bite, not wanting to eat the whole orange at once. It tasted old and awful. I pulled a face and swallowed the gritty paste in my mouth.

"I don't want it," I said, holding the orange up to my mother. "It doesn't taste right."

She took it from me and popped it in her mouth. She was wearing lipstick. Bright coral. My mother never wore lipstick. "It tastes fine," she said, "It's marzipan, made from almonds. It's supposed to taste like that."

"I thought it would taste like oranges," I said.

"Don't be silly. How could it? It's marzipan." And she went back to staring out the window. I was hurt and pulled on Chatty Cathy's ring. "Let's play school," she said. At least someone was talking to me.

"It tasted funny," I said to Chatty Cathy. "It wasn't a nice taste at all."

I had been promised an adventure: a nice train ride, a visit with *Tante* Edda, and a trip to the sea. This wasn't a nice train ride. My mother was acting strange. I didn't like it.

"When can we go home?" I asked her. "I miss everyone." I didn't particularly want to go home, but I had discovered that this question was a good way to get attention. Usually it made her circle me with her arms and smooth my hair, and tell me what a good *kind* I was.

"Not yet," she answered crossly. "We have things to do first."

This was not the expected response and I began to cry. Little tears.

"What's wrong now?" she asked me, clearly impatient.

"I don't like this," I said. "I want to go home."

"*I* am home," she said, "this is *my* home. Don't you want to be here with me? We're going to the sea. You will meet *Tante* Edda whom I love very much. She has a big house near the sea. She had a little girl once. Her name was Maartje."

"That's a stupid name," I said, but then, because my mother looked so annoyed, I continued, "tell me about Maartje—what happened to her?"

And my mother began the story of *Tante* Edda and *Ome* Hendrik, and Maartje and the terrible time near the end of the war when there was nothing to eat but herring and shrimp and no eggs and no vegetables because the soldiers had taken everything, and how Maartje became weaker and weaker, and her little legs became so thin that she couldn't stand on them and had to lie down on the bed all day long, and how she just faded away and died and there was nothing to be done. And I fell asleep while she was talking, and when I woke up she was shaking me and the train was had stopped.

The train conductor lifted me down off the train, grabbing me easily under my arms and swinging me in the air. It was fun. But I worried that someone might see my underpants. When he put me down, I pulled up my white knee socks and stood still, waiting for my mother to join me. She was carrying our small suitcase. Heavy brown cardboard with leather corners and a handle, lined with brown-checked cotton. I thought it was very ugly. My mother looked like a stranger. She was wearing black pumps and dark taupe nylons, and carrying a matching black bag from Eaton's. I hated the taupe nylons. She looked very nice, but she didn't look like my mother. She was smiling broadly and speaking to people in Dutch as we walked through the train station. The station was big and dirty and noisy. I didn't like it.

"Now," she said to me, "we take the tram." I followed her, Chatty Cathy under my arm and a little white straw purse clutched in my hand. Inside my purse were my Sunday gloves, a white handkerchief with red strawberries stamped on it, a little coin purse, and a white plastic case with my rosary bunched up inside. These were the things that a lady carried in her purse. My mother had taught me this.

We took the tram for a long ride out to the edge of the city. My mother seemed to know where we were going, and she became quite animated, speaking with people on the tram and introducing me to strangers. I was embarrassed by this and looked down at my shoes in shame. When we got off the tram, my mother waved merrily at our fellow passengers before descending the few steps to the street level. The driver called something out to her in Dutch. I was sullen. She was beaming. Grabbing my arm, she pulled me along the cobbled street to a tall brick row house. The front door was painted shiny black and there was a huge brass lion knocker on it. She let me bang it. The door opened immediately, and two old people came out onto the street and wrapped themselves around my mother. The three of them locked together and cried and spoke excitedly in Dutch. They forgot about me entirely. I watched them with some amazement.

We all went into the house after a few minutes and after I had endured three kisses each from *Tante* Edda and *Ome* Hendrik. First one side of the cheek, then the other, and back again to the first. *Ome* Hendrik smelled funny. It was a sweet, fruity, smoky smell. *Tante* Edda was dressed in black and looked very old and very serious. They scared me. Mother said I could play in the dining room while they visited, and I was plunked alone in a large room with Chatty Cathy, a glass of milk, and a plate of cookies. I was tired, so I sat down on the carpet to study the intricate pattern and eventually fell asleep. When I woke up, the three of them were standing beside me and laughing. I was indignant. Mother said it was time to go to the sea. We left our suitcase, my purse, and my doll. Mother took my hand in hers, and we held hands and walked to the sea.

"*Poffertjes!*" exclaimed my mother, leading me toward a small red-and-white-striped tent. "We must have *poffertjes*." I watched silently while my mother ordered, and the man tipped a scoop of round baked cake things into paper bags and dusted them generously with icing sugar. They were still warm and dissolved quickly in my mouth. They were good. My mother was delighted.

"I knew you'd like them," she said.

She was leading me to a large sandy hill, and I was getting sand in my shoes. She noticed my trouble and pulled me along a little further until there was no one around us. "Take off your shoes and socks and carry them," she said. To my amazement, she did the same. She lifted her skirt, undid the buttons on her garter belt, rolled down her nylons, and took off her shoes. She laughed at me. "Don't be so serious," she said, "we're at the sea."

And, without waiting, my mother ran along the sand, climbed the hill, and waved at me. "Come on," she called, "climb the dyke." I ran after her.

"Where's the dyke?" I asked when I reached her.

"You're standing on it," she said. "They don't all look like the ones in your book. Most of them look like this one—large dunes."

"But where did the boy stick his finger?" I asked. I was remembering the story of the Dutch boy who saved Holland by plugging a hole in the dyke with his finger.

"They're not all like that, I told you," replied my mother. She was now headed down the other side of the dyke, having taken off her jacket and placing it, with her purse, shoes, and stockings rolled neatly beside it, into a small pile. Her pale pink nylon blouse, buttoned at the back, had come untucked from her skirt band. She began to run.

I followed, carrying my shoes and socks. When I caught up with her she was wading in the sea. I crossed a wide border of white-and-blue shells, to join her. They felt wiggly and unsteady under my feet. Some of them were sharp. My mother didn't notice. She didn't caution me. She was ankle-deep in water, running her hands through her tightly-permed black hair. I went to stand beside her. She splashed water at me with her hands. My dress got wet. "Mom! What are you doing?"

"Having fun! For the first time in years, I'm having fun."

She left me standing in the shallows and ran down the beach, kicking and splashing, and picking up shells. I stayed behind and sulked. I watched her small pile of clothes to make sure nobody came and took them. After what seemed like a very long time, she returned to me. She was smiling. She took my hand, and we walked back to the pile of her belongings. She put on her shoes and placed her nylons in her purse. She snapped the clasp shut. She tucked in her blouse, put on her jacket, and did up all the buttons. She smoothed and patted her hair. She did not talk to me. She had a faraway look about her that I did not recognize.

We walked back to *Tante* Edda's house. I slept in a closet in the wall. A small bed concealed behind heavy curtains. It was Maartje's bed. Nobody had slept in it since she died. I was allowed to play with her dolls. They were lined up in a white wicker doll pram. My mother told me that I had to put them back exactly the way I found them. They stared at me, wide-eyed, when I climbed up into the closet bed. Chatty Cathy came into the bed with me. I had dressed her in her nightgown while I readied myself for bed. I pulled her ring. "May I have a cookie?" was all she had to say about things.

The next morning, my mother, wearing her ugly suit, went walking about town by herself. I had to stay with *Tante* Edda and *Ome* Hendrik. In the morning, I played with Maartje's dolls. In the afternoon, *Ome* Hendrik pulled a ladder down from the ceiling and I followed him upstairs to the attic. Upstairs was a playroom with a rocking horse, a bookshelf, and a swing hanging from the rafters. He told me in his broken *Engels* that I could *spelen* here. Dinner that night consisted of my *Tante's* specialty: *croquettes*. I had never eaten them before and they burned my mouth. The texture was creamy inside, like mashed peas, but the outside was a hard breadcrumb crust.

We ate them with applesauce for dinner. Then we had stewed fruit and custard for dessert. It was a strange meal. My mother enjoyed it. She talked non-stop all through the meal and made *Tante* Edda and *Ome* Hendrik laugh a lot. She had spent the day visiting with people she hadn't seen since she had left to join my father in Canada ten years before. They still remembered her. That's all I understood. The rest was in Dutch and it was too much trouble to focus and try to understand.

After dinner, I stayed in the dining room and played with my Barbie. My mother had packed her in the brown cardboard suitcase, and this had surprised me. Barbie had a very extensive wardrobe, and I spent the evening happily changing her dresses and shoes. The grown-ups were drinking and laughing loudly when I went to bed in the strange wall closet. Other relatives had come to visit, and the house was filled with laughter and loud happy voices. I had been introduced to all of these people, but they were old with funny names like Joop and Case, and I wasn't very comfortable with any of them.

My mother left me again the next day. *Ome* Hendrik offered to take me for a bicycle ride to the park, but I had seen the bicycles riding quickly through the streets, weaving in and out of traffic, and I was afraid to try. He shrugged his shoulders at this and went out into the backyard to weed the vegetable garden and smoke his pipe. I was lonely, bored, and not a little miffed that my mother was out visiting while I was left alone with these two old people. When she came home at night, I planned to tell her that I wanted to go home.

But I did not say this to her when she returned. She seemed unhappy. I listened to her speaking to *Tante* Edda in the kitchen before supper, but I could not make out the words. That evening, there was more company. But this time the mood was serious. Something was being discussed in earnest. Nobody came to tuck me in. Chatty Cathy told me that she loved me.

It was not long after this that mother said to me that we were going home. "The Netherlands has nothing for me anymore," was how she concluded her announcement. She began to cry. *Tante* Edda put her hand on my mother's shoulder. That afternoon, *Ome* Hendrik walked us to the tram stop. Before we got on the tram, he handed me a small paper bag. Seated on the tram, I opened the bag and pulled out the contents. Inside I found a large pink marzipan pig, and a handful of small marzipan fruits. I was disappointed. My mother looked at the marzipan and at my face.

"You will come to love it someday," she said, "just not now. Nothing makes sense now."

We flew home and were greeted at the airport by my brothers and father. We drove in our red-and-white Beaumont, and I chatted happily with my brothers. They teased me a little. In the front seat, my parents sat stiffly. They had not embraced or kissed. My father had on his angry face. My mother was wearing a plain navy blue dress. No hat. No lipstick. The marzipan pig and fruit were put on my dresser, and left there until they became dusty. I would not eat them, but did not want to throw them out either. When the fighting started late at night, behind closed doors, I would pick them up and poke at them until they became marked all over by my thumbnails. I was sure that the marzipan somehow contained the secret of my mother's unhappiness and of the unexplained trip we had taken. I wanted desperately to be able to bite into the fruit and savour the taste of it, believing that, if I could do so, all would be restored, and my mother would become forever as she was that one day at the sea.

Garden Story

HIS SHYNESS SIMPLY BAFFLED HER at first. Over time, she had come to understand that he had not known how to absorb another into the rhythm of a life already established. And then he invited her to see his garden. Deep in the ravine, adjacent to the house, and unknown to her entirely, was the quiet and grace of a cool green room, with shaded rocks and hostas and mosses. A hollow deep in the corner hid a tiny stream of water that ran along split bamboo and dropped softly into a half-hidden concrete basin. A bird splashed there while the fading sun spotted the pebbles and plants with a gentle, filtered light. He led her there, walking quietly on the bark humus, gently pushing aside moist leaves, while she passed closely behind. The dull sounds of nearby traffic were no longer audible at this remove, and, although she had strained to hear, the trees muffled the city noises and kept them securely enveloped in the midst of all that was verdant and tranquil.

Bending, he reached to pick her a delicate bouquet of fuscia *Phlox* and white *Dicentra*. Later, she would learn that *Phlox* was a native plant and that the common name for *Dicentra* was *Bleeding Heart*. Carrying the flowers on her way up the embankment she repeated the Latin name silently, practicing the feel of it in her mouth. *Dicentra*. The garden was a world of rare names and fragrances. It was still and alluring, and she realized that it was a place that she had longed for, without knowing what words to put to her need. He was waiting for her at the terrace, drinks already poured, and they stayed there until nightfall talking.

He invited her again and she went. They planted bulbs together: *Galanthus* and *Muscari* and *Scilla*. They spoke in hushed tones and listened to the bird calls. When the *Lupin*s were spent, they cradled the dry pods in cupped hands and sowed the seeds. Carefully they watered, pushing the tiny grains into the earth with muddy fingers. Their days became measured by a passion for the place that she had come gradually to share, and no day ended without a walk to see all that was new and changing.

They worked silently in the fall of their first year together, wary of winter and wondering what task would mark their time when the ground was frozen and snow covered. But the cold months had passed, and she had found a place with him in front of the fire with delicate sherry glasses and glossy magazines. Together they planned for spring, anticipating luminous green shoots, longing to greet the bright bulbs and the strong perennials. And then one night, wrapped in quilts, they stood shivering on the terrace to watch a shooting star. Above the ravine, it blazed a trail in the dark.

Acknowledgements

Many thanks to Inanna Publications and especially to Luciana Ricciutelli, Editor-in-Chief, and Kimberley Griffiths, Editorial Assistant, for their support and effort to shepherd me through this process.

My deepest gratitude to Donna Morrissey for her friendship, loving heart, and constant encouragement.

With thanks also to Antanas Sileika and David Bezmozgis for their leadership at the Humber College School of Writing and for all that they do to develop new writers.

I am so grateful to Emma Louise Oram, Joy Barratt, Wendy Bentley, Marilyn and Dallas Black for listening to my stories.

And finally, to the people of Cartwright Township who welcomed us and helped me to find a voice.

Versions of the following stories were previously published as follows:

"South End" previously published in *under the gum tree*, January 2013.

"The Wages of Sin" was shortlisted for the Bridport Prize,

2015; a finalist for the Ian MacMillan Award; and received an honourable mention in The Short Story Ireland contest, 2014.

"A Love Story" previously published by *The Antigonish Review*, Number 184, 2015.

"A Hawk in Winter" published in a *Rubery Anthology* in 2015. Third Prize winner, International Rubery Short Story Competition, 2014.

"Oliver Hambley" previously published in *Vintage Script*, Issue 10, Summer 2013.

"The Yellow House" previously published in *Vintage Script*, Issue 9, Spring 2013.

"The Shoe Tree" previously published in *Gargoyle Magazine*, Vol. 60, 2013.

"Gridlock" previously published in *Flash 101*, Vol. 5, Fast Forward Press, 2012.

"Mrs. Harris" previously published in *under the gum tree*, July 2014.

"Romaine Hearts" previously published in *Forge*, Vol.7, Issue 1, Summer 2013.

"The Canadian Shield" previously published online in *Temenos Journal*, Winter 2013.

"Creamers" previously published in *Hawai'i Review*, Issue 78, Spring 2013.

ACKNOWLEDGEMENTS

"The Marzipan Fruit Basket" previously published in *Cyphers*, Issue 71, Spring 2011.

"Garden Story" previously published online in *Romance Magazine*, Vol. 2, No.10, November 2014.

Photo: Jonathan van Bilsen

Lucy E. M. Black is an educator. She studied creative writing at the undergraduate level and earned an M.A. in nineteenth-century British fiction. Her short stories have been published in many publications including *Cyphers Magazine, under the gum tree, the Hawai'i Review, Vintage Script*, and the *Antigonish Review*. She lives with her husband in a small town near Toronto, Ontario. *The Marzipan Fruit Basket* is her debut collection of short fiction.